THE ODYSSEY OF IZ

CRISTINA KESSLER

CRISTINA KESSLER

Book cover design by Frank Welffens
Izdihar is illustrated by Cincinart (Olga Matyash)

ACKNOWLEDGMENTS

There are many folks I would like to thank for making this book possible. First, to the love of my life and first editor, Joe, whose constant encouragement keeps me writing. Also, to Frank Welffens, my Creative Director on this project for his unwavering support and expertise. Thanks to three early readers, Trisha and Vicki, and to Paulette Nichols who was with me on a pirogue trip down the Niger River. This is my first self-published young adult novel with no agent or editor, and so I hope it inspires my readers that want to write to just go for it.

AUTHOR'S NOTE

Early marriage and girls' education are two topics that have been on my mind for years. As Peace Corps Volunteers in the Seychelles in 76-78, I did a six-month program for the UN Fund for Population Activities, and surveyed locals on everything from birth control practices to girls' education to early marriage. Then when we lived in Ethiopia years later, I saw early marriage taken to the extreme.

I decided to write **The Odyssey of Iz** from a young girl's perspective that could address both issues, early marriage, and education. My character was named for my Sudanese friend and masseuse, Izdihar, where we lived for 2 years and 8 months in the late 90's. Izdihar was a young woman from Khartoum, pursuing a profession that was very unusual. Izdihar had to fight with her parents to follow her dream. Her story of determination, crossing cultural boundaries and pursuing her dream inspired me to write this book.

Like all of my young adult novels and picture books, this one is based on numerous experiences taken directly from my journals. Madame N'Dour of Senegal was my neighbor in Mali. Her powers were evident to me from early on and although all we had in common was a shared wall we did eventually evolve into friends, sharing what was one of Iz's discoveries, the importance of mutual respect.

The Wodabbe and Fulani celebrations are events embedded in my memory bank. To see men adorn themselves and dance with great enthusiasm to attract a wife was a real departure from normal African - even world practices. Another situation far from her reality, provided Bella with the opportunity to tell Iz, different isn't good or bad, better, or worse, it's just different. Seeing the cattle cross a river was also an unforgettable sight. My friend, Paulette Nichols, and I hired a tiny 10-foot pirogue, carved from a single log, and three crewmen to paddle us 1000 miles down the Niger River. We almost went over a dam and had hippo encounters and wonderful experiences with our boat men Hassan, the singer and tea maker riding stern, and Musa, the go-to-guy who always had a ready smile and lots of energy. Fortunately, we had no close call of Musa drowning.

Karim and Omar were created to help me spread the word about the gentle side of Islam. These two religious scholars discuss everything from war to arranged marriage.

Iz likes them a lot until Omar offers his 14-year-old daughter to 26-year-old Karim. Izdihar's outrage about the arranged marriage creates a real rift between Iz and her guide/teacher/friend/fellow traveler, Bella. Bella is a chevron bead she finds on the desert the night she learns that she will be married soon to a stranger, and all of her dreams of studying and being a doctor are suddenly cancelled. Sitting on the desert sand as night falls, pounding the ground while screaming, "I will not get married to an old man! Not now! Not ever!" her pounding uncovers a rare chevron trade bead, called the aristocrat of beads. Izdihar picks it up and admires its beauty and knows its old and been around, so she says, "If only you could talk and take me on the travels that brought you here, that would solve my immediate problems." And in the flash of a lightning bolt the adventure begins.

Bella and Iz form a team that has them laughing, fighting, glaring, loving, and always talking. Their travels are made possible by being invisible so the bead, that Iz names Bella, can take her back to all her owners, trades, good times, and bad times. Their relationship is the way Bella teaches her about the shortcomings of being judgmental, the advantages of leading by example rather than demands, the beauty of the countries they visit, the joy of having an open mind, and the realization that war is not new.

I truly hope that my readers gain a greater understanding of how different each African country is, and similar too. I hope they stop and think about how many times they have dismissed something because it was so unfamiliar. I hope they open their minds to all different ways of life, and appreciate that just because it's not their way, it's not automatically wrong. Travel does that for an individual, and since travel has become so difficult in these times, why not do it through a book? I hope my readers enjoy their time in 7 different countries, numerous new cultures, learning about all the things that can make the world better, and that it should be as easy to offer mutual respect as it is to spread disdain. Especially now.

Bottomline, I hope they love this book like I do! And if I ever meet a reader, I will be sure to share with them my chevron bead, Bella, that I have treasured and carried with me for 30 years!

THE ODYSSEY OF IZ

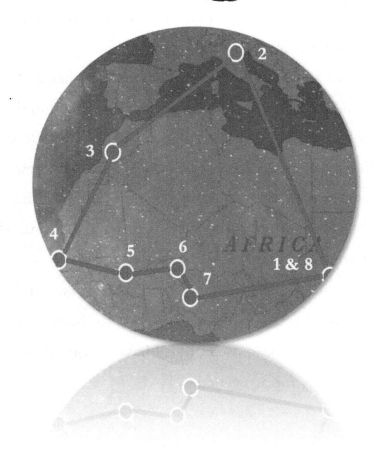

1– Sudan
2– Murano, Italy
3– Marrakech, Morocco

4– N'Dar, Senegal
5– Walk to Niger River Crossing
6– Niger River Trip

7– Nigeria
8– Sudan

My *Haboob* Girl

It started with tiny little dust devils, spinning on the horizon. They quickly grew into giant whirling cones of red dust, taller than any of the giant old baobab trees dotting the desert's distance. Izdihar watched with all her attention, taking in the solid wall of dust building skyward behind the twisting dust devils. And then it arrived. The loose end of Izdihar's faded blue *towb* slapped her in the face as the wind raced around her.

It came from the north with such sudden force that straw from the rooftops was torn away and sent tumbling every which way across the family's compound. Izdihar's teeth filled with grit as she smiled into the giant dust storm. The date palm trees bent over sideways, their shadows disappearing in the red darkness that moved over them.

"It's the *haboob*," yelled her father as he hung tightly onto his turban. "Run for cover!"

Izdihar charged toward the hut, where she stopped at the door to watch the action. One minute the sun was pouring down its full heat, and the next it was dark, like late dusk, rather than early afternoon. Her blue robe whipped around her, flapping like a little flag in a big wind.

"Come in you silly girl," cried her mother as she grabbed Izdihar's *towb* to tug her inside. "What makes you so foolish?"

Izdihar stumbled as she fell through the narrow doorway, skinning her elbow on the hard, dry mud wall. She ran to the window hole to watch the power of Mother Nature. She loved the desert, for there was no buffer zone or quiet space between her and the elements. When it was hot, which was most of the year, she sweated through her clothes like all the rest. And when the cold season came for four wonderful months she shivered like the rest when the temperature dropped down into the 80's.

As she watched, the wall of dust became so thick she could no longer see her father who was running toward the hut. What she did see was his turban fly past the window, within her reach if she could have reacted fast enough. But it was gone, and she said to herself as it disappeared from her view, "I wish I could fly like that."

Tonight, she thought, the desert will be wonderful. The old will have been swept away by the great *haboob* broom, and the desert floor will be a new collection of things to investigate. She jumped when her father raced through the door. His head wore a cap of dust, and his white robe was streaked with a fine layer of red stripes — the color of the desert. His smile shined brightly in his dirty face.

"You and the wind," her father laughed. "I should call you my *haboob* girl."

As suddenly as it had come, the wind died down. Izdihar and her father walked outside, where the sky was a solid red cloud, the sun a weak silhouette in the curtain of suspended red dust that filled the air. It looked as if someone had placed a giant bowl over the earth, with the dimmed light, and the ground and the sky exactly the same colors.

"It's beautiful," said Izdihar as she spun a slow circle to take in the full horizon. She caught sight of her mother, coming out the door. Her little sister Fanta rested on her mother's hip.

"You're right, it is beautiful. But do you know what would really be beautiful? What would be beautiful is to see you finish your chores," said her mother.

"You're right too," said Izdihar, for she had plans. She grabbed the empty bucket made of an old tire and headed to the well, planning the desert walk she would take later. The afternoon loomed long as she thought of all her chores. She was eager to finish and scour the new desert floor, swept by the strong *haboob*.

Izdihar worked the afternoon away, feeling as if her work dragged on forever. Finally, she headed-off to her final job before dinner. With her baby sister Fanta snuggled onto her back tucked beneath a bright yellow cloth, and a basket on her head that threw a pool of shade before her, Izdihar walked slowly toward the animal's watering hole to collect cow and camel dung for the fire.

Desert Treasure

The well stood apart from the village and was always busy with boys hauling water and animals drinking and flies buzzing. As she walked slowly toward it Izdihar pulled a folded piece of paper from her sleeve. Stopping in her tracks she carefully unfolded the deeply creased paper, and then looked around casually. The basket balanced perfectly on her rotating head, as she checked to see if anyone was watching her. Seeing only a boy leading the camel pulling water from the well, and another boy filling the troughs surrounded by goats and cows and camels, she held the paper up over her shoulder.

"Look Fanta, my greatest desert treasure. I found this after a *haboob* two years ago, long before you were born. It was a *haboob* as strong as the one today. Who knows what waits for me on the desert tonight?"

She held the creased paper, worn soft with much handling, in front of her and said, "Look, a map of the world." Then lifting the furrowed paper high again to show Fanta she said, "My teacher showed me where Sudan lies," as her finger lightly traced the orange shape of Sudan. "We are the largest country in Africa."

Then drawing a line northwest, she told her quiet little sister, "I want to go here. To London. The radio says they have women doctors there, and that's what I want to be." In the muted, dusty light left behind by the day's *haboob* the colors on the map were still brilliant, each country a distinct color from its neighbors. Every time Izdihar looked at the photo, and no one could count how many times that had been, she saw something new. It was a page cut from a magazine that had been tossed across the sandy plains by a great desert wind. Izdihar had found it, quite far from the sand track used by passing busses and trucks loaded with passengers. It was her greatest desert treasure.

Looking toward the horizon she told sleeping Fanta, "Ah little sister, thanks to you I know I want to be a doctor."

She had not forgotten one detail of her little sister's birth. Her mother had entered her labor early, and the only midwife for miles was with another mother in need. Izdihar's father sent her brother to find a neighbor, then set-off at a pace faster than a dust devil to find the midwife and let her know his wife's time had arrived. While he was gone, Fanta had decided to leave the safety of her mother's womb and enter the world.

As if her mother wasn't busy enough with the pains that gripped her with every contraction, she had to tell her frightened and amazed daughter Izdihar what to do step by step. Remembering out loud, Izdihar told her sleeping sister, "I remember begging you to stay inside just a bit longer, until real help could arrive, but you wouldn't. Mother told me where to get the soft washed cloth to welcome you, and the clean knife to cut the cord of life."

Izdihar was proud of herself for helping her mother in such a great time of need. She had thought she would faint at first, with all the blood and pain, but what happened was she became more focused than she had ever been in her 13 short years. She caught her little sister and announced to her mother, "Allah has given us another girl." She was so intent on what to do next that she didn't hear the midwife arrive and was surprised when the woman touched her shoulder and said, "Let me finish here. You have done a wonderful job."

Popping back into the present Izdihar said, "It's because of you I want to become a doctor, to help all in the village one day. And because of Omar." Stroking the map again and again she told Fanta, "But I want to travel and see the world before then." She touched Asia, and America and Europe. "I want to know life here and here and here. All dreams that look impossible right now, for we live in a place where all daughters follow in the footsteps of their mothers and all the mothers before them."

Fanta sighed against her sister's back, then kicked her little feet like a puppy in a dream. Izdihar tapped her bottom and said, "Don't get me wrong - the world needs mothers. Anyway, how can I go and leave you? And mother who keeps me so busy, or father and his flying turban? I might even miss our spoiled brother Khalil, though it's hard to imagine that."

She thought of the giant planes, far up in the sky that she had seen twice. The first time she had watched in awe, her mouth dropping open. Her father stood at her side and laughed when he saw her face. "It's an airplane," he said "full of many people flying somewhere far away. Your Uncle Yussuf took one to make the *hajj* journey to Mecca." Her father had shaken his head and said, "He still brags about it. He says they were served food and tea as they flew along. Not all planes go to Mecca. Where they go or why they go I cannot tell you."

"Go" was really the only word she heard that day more than two years before. Now, smoothing her hand across the world map she said, "But I do know that travel I must." Pointing to Alaska she wistfully said, "I'm sure no one there is collecting dung," which reminded her of what she was supposed to be doing. Quickly but carefully, she folded the shiny sheet along its familiar creases, and put it back up her dress sleeve under her old blue *towb*.

Hurrying off to an area where there were no animals, she pulled the basket from her head and dropped it to the ground. She picked up the driest plops of dung from the dirt and threw them at the basket, bending and straightening and muttering all the while.

"Get the dung."

"Take care of your sister."

"Watch your brother."

"Bring the water."

"Sweep the compound."

"Pound the millet."

And with a toss of the biggest dung pie yet she released a heavy sigh.

Just then Fanta whimpered, and Izdihar reached around to pat her tiny little bottom again and said, "Sorry little sister, I forgot you were there. Let's get this work done and go home."

Noticing how long the shadows had become, she realized she was a long time getting the dung together. Rushing back, basket on her head and baby on her back, Izdihar worried about her mother being angry. She couldn't imagine not going out into the desert this evening, especially right after a big *haboob*. But if her mother were angry, she could and she would forbid it.

Desert walks were what Izdihar lived for. As she walked, she always wondered what lay beyond the next sand dune. What it looked like where the sun sinks each evening. But the biggest question of all was always the same, would she ever leave her small desert village where everyone knew everyone else, and all their business too? The picture of the map, so fresh in her mind, made her more determined to leave one day.

The Dream

Dinner was the same as usual, *fuul* beans and thick bread. Izdihar looked around the family circle as they ate. Her father sat tall, never spilling a drop or a bean on his white gown as he moved the food from the tray to his mouth. His dark smooth skin fit his face perfectly, Izdihar thought again as she looked at him. A black beard hugged his chin and upper lip.

Her brother, Khalil, leaned forward with his right hand, stretching across the giant platter. Her mother slapped his wrist gently and said, "Eat from the place in front of you. What makes you reach across the platter so rudely? Is this what I have raised, a boy with no manners?"

Embarrassed, Khalil said, "I just wanted that tomato there, next to the chunk of onion. But this looks fine here," and he dipped his bread and scooped a large mouthful of the brown beans.

She watched her family, as if from afar, and thought, "*I wonder if they will miss me?*" She had decided on her walk home that she would study hard, so that when she was old enough for university she would leave, to study medicine. And not only would she study hard, but she would start talking of her plans frequently so that her parents might begin to share the dream.

Unfortunately, the idea had not gone over well when she told her parents about her plans to go to university and become a doctor. It was just after Fanta's birth, so 11 moons had passed since she last mentioned her dream.

Her mother had snorted and said, "Where do you get such silly ideas? A woman doctor?" Tilting her head, she had added, "You did well when I needed you most, so why not be a midwife, delivering babies and having your own, right here?"

Her father just gently shook his head back and forth, asking, "And where will we get the money for such an education? No, I am sorry, but you should not make dreams you cannot realize." Gazing at his wife, Father said, "Your mother is right. A midwife is an honorable and attainable profession."

She had dropped the subject, as conversation, but kept it alive in her head. She didn't know how or when, but she did know she would be a doctor one day. She wanted more skills than a midwife had, to be able to help all in her village. She knew that if there had been a doctor in the village her youngest brother Omar would probably still be alive.

The midwife had tried her best, but when it was clear that only a quick operation could save him, and there was no one within half a day with the skills and knowledge, he had passed. It was almost as if he had never existed, for no one spoke of him, the pain still too great for all in the family. Izdihar knew in her heart not to mention Omar as her reason for being a doctor – not yet anyway. There had only been one dry season since his passing, and the pain still gripped each person's heart.

Too many memories, she thought. A voice in her head brought her back to the moment, telling her, "Right now though, you need to get out to the desert and see what the *haboob* has brought you."

Izdihar helped clean up after dinner, which really only meant washing off the big round serving platter. When the large dish was back where it belonged, tucked beneath the pile of cooking pots and washing rags, Izdihar put on her favorite *towb* and headed quietly around the corner of the hut.

"Izdihar," called her mother, "where do you think you are you going? It is nearly night."

"Oh Mother, I am just going on a short walk. The

moon is full tonight and the evening cool. I won't be long," she answered as she fiddled with the long black and green cloth wrapped round her body.

"Why do you always go alone? Have you no friends?" her mother asked.

"The desert is my friend," she answered, and then hurried away as her mother shouted, "Well go tonight, for soon this foolishness will end — *khalas.*" Finished. Izdihar froze, then whipped around to face her mother and asked, "Why Mama, what do you mean?"

"Your father has put off again and again telling you, so I shall do it myself. You will be married, soon, to Jamal. Soon, and so walk if you must, for that shall end with your marriage."

"Married?" Izdihar shook her head, a small frown breaking lose across her face. "I cannot marry. I'm still at school. I'm going to be a doctor. I have things to do."

"Things to do?" laughed her mother. "Are you still talking that foolishness about being a doctor? I told you already, be a midwife if you must be more than a mother. But right now, the only thing you need to do is get married and bring us a fine dowry." Her mother slapped at a mosquito near her face, then said, "So walk my dear, if you must, for tonight is the last time. You must start to act like a young bride. And that shall start tomorrow."

Izdihar left in a daze. She walked around the corner of the compound, and then broke into a run. She ran and ran, in a straight line, toward the setting sun that had dipped down into the lingering wall of dust. The top of the sky overhead was a mellowing blue, with streaks of feathery white clouds. When the sun departed over the edge of the earth the white clouds and hanging dust curtain turned a fiery orange. Izdihar stopped suddenly, panting as she looked east and west, oblivious to the stunning sunset colors building.

She took her head in her hands, looking at her feet. With a firm shake of her shoulders she said aloud, "And so I must leave tonight. My last night of freedom."

Then standing taller, she said with determination, "I can't get married. To an old man. Not now, not ever. I am going to be a doctor." She collapsed to the ground in a flow of tears, crying with her whole body. Her sobs hung on the heavy desert air. When the tears had dried, she threw her head back and yelled at the darkening sky tinted with moonlight, smacking the desert floor with each shout. "I will not get married! Not! Not! NOT!" Her repeated smacks dug a small hole into the sand, and she stopped with a sudden "Ouch!" flinching at an unexpected hardness beneath her hand. A beautiful shape caught her eye, lying just below surface of the white sand. She slid her finger under it, and out popped a bead.

It was without a doubt the most beautiful trade bead she had ever seen. She picked it up, holding it between her thumb and forefinger to appreciate the fine lines and deep colors. As she gazed upon it, she whispered, "You're just like the bead mother always talks about. The bead mother only saw once as a small child, but never forgot. The bead that belonged to her great-grandfather." Placing it between her two palms and rolling it gently back and forth she said, "If only you could talk and take me on your travels that brought you here. That would end my problems." And in the flash of a lightning bolt everything in Izdihar's life changed.

Molta Bella

Izdihar shook her head in confusion as she looked around her. Gone were the desert sands, stretching away in all directions. Gone were the distant rolling dunes and leaning date palm trees. Gone were her village and family. Instead, she sat in a tiny, bright room, surrounded by glass and heat, watching a very handsome young man hold something up to the light.

He twisted it to the left, and the rays of the afternoon sun danced on a lovely, rounded, barrel-shaped bead resting on his palm.

"*Molta bella*," said the young man. "This is definitely my finest chevron ever. It's a masterpiece by the master bead maker, me, Luigi Grapitti." Holding it between his finger and thumb Izdihar saw that it looked just like the one she had found in the desert.

Izdihar shook her head again and said as she looked around, "Where am I, and how do I get home? My mother will be worried and terribly angry if I am late."

Luigi jumped at the sudden sound of the young girl's voice. "How did you get here?" he stammered. "And where did you come from?" Shaking his head in confusion he asked, "How long have you been here?" He could see that Izdihar was upset, so he held out the bead and said, "Look at this beautiful bead I just made."

He placed it in her palm and Izdihar gazed at its beauty. She knew in her gut that it was the same bead she had just found on the desert in Sudan. Its shape resembled the watermelon that grew for two months a year - wide in the middle and narrow at the ends. From a white core, seven layers of starburst colors followed one another – blue, white, blue, white, red, white, blue. Perfect, delicate matching lines filled the topsides of the bead.

She handed it back to Luigi, who placed it in his breast pocket. With the slightest of hesitation, she asked him, "Where am I?" Before he could answer she stared at her clothes. Instead of her *towb* she wore a dress that was tight across her chest, then flared out like her father's robe filled with wind. A finely woven white cloth covered her head and hung down to her shoulders. Her well-defined torso made her flush with embarrassment. She ran her hands over her dress and felt the desert bead in her deep pocket. The bead that looked exactly like the one Luigi had shown her. Uncertain whether or not to show him her bead she asked him with fear filling her voice, "Where am I? And what is the year?"

"You are on the secret island of Murano, Italy, home to the world's finest glass bead makers," a gruff voice said. "What is wrong with you? And the year is the same as when we left the house this morning, 1769."

Izdihar spun around to see a man rushing in the door. He was stocky, with a top hat and a vest of many colors. His mustache swept across his face, like a giant bush tamed into two points that tickled his cheeks. His long coat, heavy for the hot afternoon, filled the small workshop with the smell of sweaty wool.

With his hand outstretched he said to Luigi, "*Buongiorno*, and how is your day?"

Luigi would have answered, but he never got a chance. Without stopping to breathe, the man grabbed Luigi's hand and carried on. "I sir, am *Signor* Castelli, world trader of many different goods. Beads are my specialty, just as they are yours.

Bowing to Izdihar he said, "And this is my granddaughter, Izdihar. We are together because her mother, father, brothers, grandmother are all gone – all victims of a heartless plague."

He patted stunned Izdihar's hand and said, "She may

only be a girl, but she is as smart as any boy I have ever met. And so, we shall travel and trade together and maybe she will become the world's first woman trader." He stopped for a quick breath and said, "But enough of us." Raising his hands, he swept his arms across the room and said, "And you, my friend, are Murano's best bead man, or so they all say. Show me your wares and I'll be the judge of that."

"Excuse me sir," said a timid Izdihar. "Did you just say my family is dead? Do you know my mother and father? I have only one brother and a small sister, both healthy. And my grandmother on my mother's side is alive and well." Closing her eyes, she finished in a whisper, "And I have no grandfather."

Signor Castelli raised his right hand and tilted his head to the side. "Please dear, we are conducting business here. We'll talk later, you have been confused ever since the tragedy. We can talk later." Then turning back to Luigi, he turned both hands, palms up, and said, "So my friend the bead maker, show me your best."

Luigi reached for a bead on the shelf, and then stopped short. As he leaned forward the bead in his breast pocket swung low, pulling on his shirt. Luigi put his hand over it, not sure he wanted to show the arrogant little man his newest and best bead. Instead, he picked up his best *millefiori* bead, and held it in his closed hand. Its colors were a brilliant collection of blues and greens and yellows and reds, forming the "million flowers" it was named for. Luigi had made it almost a year ago, and kept it sitting on his shelf to give him inspiration when he needed it.

Slowly opening his hand, he showed the *millefiori* bead to *Signor* Castelli, letting it roll slowly across his palm. It was a perfect round shape, no bigger than a round smooth rock Izdihar had found once in the *wadi*, the dry riverbed near her village. The bead Luigi held flashed splashes of a red star surrounded by yellow, and a green and yellow star on a field of blue. Stretching around the bead was a red sun with white points on a background surrounded by red, smaller than a grape.

Signor Castelli took the *millefiori* on his palm and rolled it from side to side. Looking Luigi in the eye he said, "It's very beautiful, *molta bella*. But it's not the best I've seen. Is this really the best that you have got?"

Luigi tapped his breast pocket again, then pulled out his best bead. With the flair of a showman, he whipped open his fist and there sat the seven-layered chevron - its colors pure, and its design of 16 points, rare to see. *Signor* Castelli was reaching inside his shirt for something, but he stopped dead when he saw the chevron.

"*Mama mia*!" he shouted. With a trembling hand he reached for the bead, and held it as Luigi had, poised between his forefinger and thumb, just like Izdihar had out in the desert. Slowly he counted the colors on the end of the bead, and whispered, "Seven layers. I have never seen such a one before."

Then he held it closer and counted the points that ran down the neck of the bead. Still in a voice filled with awe he said, "And 16 points. Truly this is a rare jewel. The aristocrat of all beads." He showed it to Izdihar and said, "We must have it!" Then he looked at Luigi and said, "Let us talk seriously my friend. For a bead this beautiful deserves a good price, for both seller and buyer."

His eyes glow just like her mother's do before a good bargaining session, thought Izdihar.

La Lucha

Izdihar turned when Luigi said, "It is not for sale." He snapped the bead from *Signor* Castelli's thick fingers and plopped it back into his pocket.

"I'll give you 66 gold sovereigns," said the anxious *signor*. Then he continued as Luigi slowly shook his head no, "And I'll add a beautiful leather box from Morocco."

Luigi didn't say a word, he just shook his head no from side to side, smiling as he finally said, "No."

"And what about a fine hippo tooth from West Africa?" asked the sweating *signor*.

Luigi's head slowed a bit, so *Signor* Castelli dug a small, red pouch of soft leather from inside his layers of coat, shirt, and vest. His movement stirred up the smell of musty sweat in the closed-up shop. Izdihar wrinkled her nose.

With a flick of his wrist the stocky man held up a perfectly shaped white tooth. It had the soft glow of ivory and was the hippo tooth he had proposed. Luigi reached for it, running the smooth warm surface across the palm of his left hand. It was broad across the bottom, as wide as the big brass buttons on his shirt. It tapered down into a thick, sharp point. Its point looked fierce as Luigi held it up to the light. He rotated it once, then handed it back to the merchant trader. Patting his pocket, he said, "I don't think so. *Grazie.*"

Signor Castelli was a determined man. He dug into his pouch again and pulled out a sight Luigi had never seen before. It was about three inches long, with a wide ring-like circle at the base supporting what looked like four pointed branches. It had the color of age already upon it, a muted off-white with streaks of brown and black running through it.

Twisting the object back and forth, the *signor* announced, "Not only will I give you 66 gold sovereigns, AND a fine leather box from Morocco, AND a hippo tooth from West Africa, but also a rare and unique ivory Dinka ring, from the Sudan, the Land of the Blacks."

Izdihar sucked in her breath in shock. She whispered to herself, "That's my country." She knew they didn't have many elephants anymore, because people killed them for their ivory to make things like that ring.

Luigi reached for the large and unusual ring, and slid it onto his forefinger, the same finger that had just recently held one end of the chevron. Glancing over at Izdihar, *Signor* Castelli said quickly, "Not only is it a beautiful ring, but also useful. The tall pieces are the tines of a comb. Go ahead, run it through your hair."

With slow, long strokes Luigi ran the comb through his tangled black ponytail. Then he pulled it through his beard, smiling as he did.

Signor Castelli moved close and almost whispered, "This, my friend, once belonged to the famous Al Hassan Ibn Mohammed Al Wezar Al Fasi."

"You mean Leo the African?" asked an amazed Luigi. "The very same my friend, the one and only. He made two trips to Sudan between 1510 and 1518, before meeting his Most Holy, Pope Leo X."

Encouraged by Luigi's interest in Leo the African, *Signor* Castelli made a hearty sweep of his arm that seemed to take in the whole island. "Just think my friend, someone else may be lucky to have a hippo tooth, but you, my friend, will be the only one to own an ivory Dinka ring that is also a comb. You can groom anywhere anytime. And you will have a direct link to Leo the African."

Handing back the Dinka ring, Luigi took the seven-layered chevron from his pocket, resting it on his right palm. Then he held out his left palm, and the *signor* put the hippo tooth on it, then holding the ring up for a good look, he placed it next to the tooth in the artist's palm. Next, he pulled another soft pouch from inside his layers, and poured 66 gold sovereigns on the workbench. "You'll have to wait for the box. I'll send my servant back with it as soon as we get home."

Luigi bounced his hands as he weighed his decision, then closed his fist around the bead. He brought it to his lips for a quick kiss, and then gave it to *Signor* Castelli.

"It is my best," he said as he dropped it into *signor's* soft hand.

"And it shall get the best, for this is a bead of kings and queens," said the happy trader.

Turning to Izdihar *Signor* Castelli said, "We will travel soon, for now I have a good collection of things to trade. Come my dear, we must get ready because we're going to Africa."

"Sudan?" asked Izdihar with a mixture of hope and fear. She realized she was enjoying her unexpected new life with this strange little man who smelled badly. And she also realized that she hadn't worried about her mother and father for quite some time. She wasn't sure if she wanted her to trip to be over already.

Signor Castelli dropped the bead into the pouch and

then tucked it snugly inside his three layers of clothes —
smack up against his sweaty chest. He hurried from the
shop, like a man with places to go.

Izdihar waved at Luigi as she followed her excited new
grandfather out of the workshop. Walking beside the fast-
moving old man she thought, I wonder if and when I'll get
home again...

Iz?

"You may laugh," said the old man, "but have you ever been seasick like you can't believe?" He held his stomach and groaned. "Just like I am now?"

"I have never even seen the sea," Izdihar answered wistfully, gazing at the strange shoes on her feet.

"What do you mean?" snapped *Signor* Castelli. "Look around you."

Izdihar gasped when she looked up. They were on a huge wooden ship, with three sails blowing in the wind that whipped the finely woven cloth around her face. The boat rode up the front of the waves it was sailing into, the bow tipping up toward the sky. Its long figurehead, below the bowsprit, was of a woman with no top and a tail like a fish. It pointed skyward, then dipped low as they moved onto the backside of the wave. The ship tipped worse than a camel sitting down, and the wind blew like the fiercest *haboob*.

She reached out for the staircase near-by and held on tightly. The young girl threw her head back and shouted with glee at the motion of the boat. The wind darted around her, and a fine spray from the sea dusted her face sweetly. She was smiling from ear to ear, when she heard the man who called himself her grandfather calling out something.

"Iz?" he shouted. "Iz?"

"Iz?" she cried over the rush of the wind and crash of the sea against the boat's hull. "Nobody calls me Iz."

"I do," he said. "You are asking many questions. 'Do you know my family?' you ask me. 'Where are we?' you ask. 'What is the year?' All questions that I can answer, when I am finished losing my stomach's contents over this handrail."

He grabbed the wooden railing and let fly all the things left in his gut. Izdihar closed her eyes and covered her ears. When she looked again, she saw the strange little man wiping his soiled hands across his woolen coat. She scrunched her face up in disgust.

"You may find me disgusting," he said as he ran his palms down his thighs. "But you won't be with me much longer so bear with me *signorina*."

Pointing at the dress pocket that held her treasured trader bead from the great *haboob*, he said, "I know you have the bead Luigi made." Holding out his palm he rolled his chevron on it, and said, "You have the bead from your present, and I hold the bead from its beginning."

Izdihar dug into her pocket and Signor Castelli screamed, "Don't take it out! Not unless you want to return home right now."

She tightened her grip on the bead in her hand deep in her dress's pocket. She was surprised when she didn't pull it out, heeding his warning. "What do you mean by that?" she asked.

"The bead, the one you found on the desert - in your time - will take you through its life, moving from hand to hand, bag to bag, pocket to pocket, in many different countries.

But it is up to you if you will travel with it, something you shouted you wanted during your screaming fit on the sands of Sudan."

He held his bead higher and rolled it back and forth on his palm. "You said you wanted to travel. And to not marry an old man. Well, I will tell you this only one time. You will travel until you show the bead to someone else, and then you will find yourself again on the sands of the Sahara Desert. As suddenly as your arrival in Italy. It is your choice."

"You mean at any moment I can return to my family?"

Somberly he nodded his head yes. "It is your decision alone. Where you go and what you see is entirely up to you."

Staring at the chevron bead in his hand he asked, "Are you ready to give up the adventure you begged for? Are you true to your words, or do you just complain?"

Iz threw her shoulders back and said, "I am not a complainer. And why should I believe you?"

"Look around you again," he said. "Is this sea not real? Did you not just visit Italy? Are these your normal doings? Your everyday life?"

Shaking her head from side-to-side Izdihar admitted, "No, not like my village life at all." She stopped rubbing the bead she was touching in her pocket, then took her empty hand out. "Why would I want to go home if I really can travel?"

"Exactly," replied Signor Castelli. "It will be interesting to see how long you last, for there will be danger and fright and fun and challenges along the way. There will be times you will not even recognize yourself."

"Like now?" asked Izdihar as she held the skirt of her dress out. It was then that she noticed how white her skin was. Rubbing her hand roughly, as if trying to wipe off the faded color of her skin, she cried, "My family will never recognize me."

Signor Castelli stilled her hands and said, "You will be yourself when you return, so stop fretting. How long you stay will show us how strong your character is, how badly you want a new life."

Izdihar looked at the bead in the old man's hand. "If I am not with you who will I be with?"

"That I will not tell you. I will only say, you will always be with the bead and whoever owns it." Cocking his head to one side he said, "I notice that your hand is empty. I take it you plan to go with me now."

Izdihar silently nodded her head yes. *Why not?* she thought. *If all I have to do is show it to someone, why not go?* "Could I die?" she asked the old man.

"Anything is possible," he replied in a serious tone.

Izdihar patted the outside of her pocket and told *Signor* Castelli, "If I want to be a doctor, then I should start accepting challenges right now." Then she added with hesitation, "Will my mother be very angry with me for leaving?"

"She won't even know you're gone," he said. "But you must be involved 100% in the new places awaiting you. In every adventure. Promise me now, or I shall send you back immediately."

Placing her hand over her heart she said, "I promise. And I will start right now."

For seven days they sailed on the high seas. If the waters were calm, they would walk the deck, and all the while *Signor* Castelli bounced the beautiful new chevron bead on his palm.

Izdihar felt great. The sky was an uninterrupted mass of blue, and the sea deep green with a white froth trailing in their wake. Dolphins surfaced just off the starboard side, frolicking in the water as fast as the swift boat moved. The wind blew in from behind them, and Iz's white flimsy cloth snapped around her head.

"Are those really live fish?" she asked, having seen only the shriveled dried ones from the Nile in the market at home. Never had she seen a dried fish as large as the ones that played next to them. She leaned over the railing of the ship, the wind whipping her and not a grain of sand filling her straight white teeth as she smiled into it.

"I hope we aren't almost there," she said. She had her head back and her lovely face pointed at the sun. Her cheekbones, as high and pronounced as her mother's, threw a small shadow across the two dimples that filled her cheeks. Starbursts of light flashed against her closed eyelids. "I think I could do this forever," she said. And then, with a sudden cringe, she thought of her mother. "I hope you're right, and my mother hasn't missed me yet," said Izdihar. Then she whispered, "*Inshallah*," under her breath.

"What was that you said?" asked the trader.

"*Inshallah – Allah willing*, my mother has not yet missed me, just like you said."

Signor Castelli shook his head sadly. "I told you, go whenever you want." Looking her straight in the eyes he said again, "I thought you were the one who wants to travel. Go home if you miss your mother. It's too bad you have no interest in the story of the beautiful chevron – in Morocco."

"Morocco," sighed Iz. "Mother will have to wait."

Trader Talk

Iz's head swiveled around at the familiar greeting, *"Salaam Aleikoum,"* peace be with you, coming from an old man seated in his small market stall. The sunlight sparkled off the gold necklaces and bracelets that hung on the wall behind him. There were earrings of fine-worked filigree gold, with strands as fine as any spider's web. The man sat on his counter, one knee bent up and supporting the arm of the hand that held his chin. His skin was wrinkled, with lines running across it like cracks in the parched earth in Izdihar's home. His soft, rust-brown face was surrounded by a wispy white beard. He covered his baldhead with a little white prayer cap embroidered with blue and yellow threads. No teeth crowded his mouth.

"Aleikoum Wasalaam," and with you, Iz answered automatically, but he didn't hear her. His eyes twinkled as he carefully stared at *Signor* Castelli. As usual the man was in a bother about something, talking too fast in a language that he had made up.

"Trader's talk, he calls it," explained the bead. "Bits of Italian, French, and Arabic mixed together, the handiest word popping out in any language. I, my beautiful self, speak it too. In fact, I speak French, Italian, Arabic, Hausa and a little English."

Izdihar's head snapped down to look at the bead she was clutching in her hand. "Did you just talk to me?" Whispering frantically, she said again, "Did you just speak?"

The bead snorted and said, "Who else would be talking to you? There is much to discuss, but now we watch and learn."

Iz shifted back to the two men talking. She could tell the talking bead was right, as a string of foreign languages spilled from *Signor* Castelli's mouth.

"*Bon giorno, cuez katir, ça va bien?*" *Signor* Castelli mumbled. His Italian followed by Arabic followed by French, made little sense – good day, very good, are you well?

The old man nodded his head to the greeting, and he pointed to two pillows on the floor. Climbing off the counter he pulled his *jalabiyah* gown down, then squatted in the same position on one of the pillows, chin in hand. He pointed to the other pillow, then at *Signor* Castelli.

The *signor* threw his coattails up and squatted down in one motion. He landed with a thud on the hard red leather

pillow, almost sliding off its shiny surface, worn smooth
with age and use. He smiled and kept nodding his head, as
if something had come loose in the back of his neck. "And
so, my friend, many years have passed."

The old man, Sheik Abdul, asked *Signor* Castelli, "And
how is the family? And how is the work and the travels?
And what have you brought me, for I have the finest of
gold for you."

The jewelry-maker clapped his hands twice, and a
young boy's head popped around the corner of the door.
"Yes Grandfather, you need something?"

"Tea, Mohammed," said the sheik. "And sweet little
balls of sesame candy. Be quick. But before you go, please
give me my toolbox."

The young boy walked behind the counter and stooped
to pull a large wooden box from the bottom shelf. It
screeched along the metal surface, surprising everyone
sitting silently in the growing warmth of the little market
stall. The beautiful gold jewelry hanging on the mud wall
sparkled in the sunlight pouring in through the narrow
door.

Izdihar watched the activity that passed the doorway.
It amazed her how much the bustling market in Marrakech,

Morocco in the 1800's reminded her of the market at home, centuries later. Goatherds were being marched through, while young boys carried trays on their heads, selling fresh bread, or oranges, or round balls of tobacco. All women flowing through the market had covered heads and long gowns, and Iz thought, that's just like at home too.

Iz walked to the door for a better look outside. Being invisible is liberating, she thought. Small stalls of wood and dung lined the narrow alleyway. Men in beautifully embroidered gowns strolled along, talking with friends as they went. A string of camels, lead by a boy her brother's age, casually walked through the heavy foot traffic and donkey carts. Their large heads with big eyes stood tall above the people, and they seemed to gaze upon all below with an arrogant stare.

Izdihar turned back to the room as the young boy set the wooden toolbox between the two seated men.

"*Shukran*," said the old man.

"You are welcome my grandfather," he replied as he left to fetch the tea. Iz and the bead watched as the old man opened the large wooden box carefully, gently lifting the lid off and placing it by his side. Next, he lifted out a set of scales that glowed brightly in the sunlight. Two small round plates hung by thin chains on either side of the pointed centerpiece. Then one by one, he lined up small discs of lead, each bigger than the one before. The weights looked like an army of sturdy little soldiers standing at attention next to the scale.

Just then the grandson entered with a large round tray carrying two small glasses of steaming dark tea and a dish of sweets. He placed the tray down in front of the *signor*, inviting him to take a glass of the hot sweet *chai*, which *Signor* Castelli did with pleasure. He held the glass high until the old Sheik lifted his glass too, then they toasted to good health, and good business.

The old gold dealer carefully laid three leather boxes on the opposite side from the waiting army of weights. With care he opened each one, then sat back to await the *signor's* offer. He was surprised when the Italian merchant said, "Only your best. I bring only the best of the best. From the island of Murano, where the finest Venetian bead makers live and work, destined to never leave the island so that the secrets of their beautiful beads remain with only them. And from the best I have brought the best."

"I love this part," said the bead. She and Iz watched as

the *signor* sat back and awaited the Moroccan man's answer. "The best you say," said the old man in the strange language the two men conversed in, "but you show me nothing." Reaching into the first leather box the old man took out a golden chain, with links as big as fishhooks.

"24 karat, pure gold," he said as he set it on one dish of the scale. The plate dropped until the old man slid two of the army discs on the opposite plate, and their weights balanced. "And 24 ounces of the absolute best gold work. Only something very special can trade for this. And I doubt you have anything special enough."

"Iz, here comes the good part," shouted the bead as *Signor* Castelli pulled his pouch from its hiding place. With an exaggerated movement he yanked open the red silk bag held closed by two long drawstrings, then reached in for the bead while staring the old man in the eye. He grasped it between his thumb and forefinger, then pulled it slowly from the bag. The old man sucked his lips clean into his mouth at the sight of the seven-layer chevron.

"*Cuez katir*," wheezed the old man. Very good!

"You're right it's very beautiful," boasted the trader from Venice.

"And you sir, are right too!" called out the bead.

Iz glanced down at the bead and asked, "You love yourself very much, don't you?"

The bead's answer was quick, "Yes I do. And why shouldn't I? But watch, for I also love this part."

Without a word the old dealer added a thick gold bracelet and two rings to the dish on the scale, but the *signor* only shook his head no, just like Luigi did back in Murano. The old gold man scratched at his hairy ear, then said, "I have what you want."

He dug into the big box again, this time pulling up a false bottom and laying the piece of wood to one side. He reached in again and brought out a gold bar from the depths of the wooden box, placing it gently on the floor in front of him. It glittered and shined in the sunlight, and even the stoic Italian trader, *Signor* Castelli, could not hide his amazement.

He lifted it, bouncing it in his upturned hand, trying so hard to be casual. He looked at it from above, and below, and then from the side, estimating the size. It was about three inches long and one inch wide, with a thickness of less than half an inch. One thing was certain, it was solid gold.

"This and the necklace," said the Italian merchant,

holding out the gold bar. "Then we will be two happy, honest men."

"That," said the old gold trader, pointing at the bar the other man held, "and these," dropping a pair of little earrings onto the gold bar.

Signor Castelli wanted the gold bar badly, but as a man of pride he had to continue the discussion. He pointed at a small ring and said, "That will finish the deal nicely. You know, only the richest of men have fine chevrons. But this is not a fine chevron, this is the finest of chevrons. No friend or enemy can ever shame you by owning a better bead."

The old man rolled the chevron on his palm, already imagining it when he would show it to Khalid the barber and Abdoulaye the goldsmith. He hated to give in first, so he put the ring back into the box, and went to pick up the earrings. With his arm in midair, he made an act of dropping the earrings back onto the gold bar and said, "Last offer. *Khalas.* Finished."

Signor Castelli picked up the gold bar and earrings. With a tip of his head he said, "May I?" He reached across and took the bead from Sheik Abdul's hand, then brought the chevron to his face and kissed it once. With flair he handed it back to Sheik Abdul. He shook the old man's hand, then stood to leave. "A good deal is when everyone is happy," said the Italian trader. "We made a good deal."

"Do you believe it?" asked the delighted bead. "I was worth more than 70 times my weight - in gold."

"Is that the most you were ever traded for?" asked Izdihar.

"*Mama mia*, no! But that, my dear, was your first good question."

"Is it good enough to get me home? Didn't you say the right question would get me home?"

"No *Cara Mia*. Just a good question but not the right question."

"What does *Cara Mia* mean?" asked Izdihar.

"My dear, most affectionately," said the bead.

"I like that," the young Sudanese girl said to herself.

"You'd better like it because now it is just you and me. No old trader, just you and me. I am taking you on the trip of my life, from owner to owner, all rich and proud to own me, but all forced to trade me for different reasons to different people. Not all will be pleasant or happy memories for me, but no one will know we are there living my life again.

"The most important thing to remember is that we must stay together. Invisible but together."

Iz drew a deep breath as she took in the odd information.

Snake

That night the old gold dealer took his new bead down to the main square, Djemma el Fna. There were people milling about in great numbers, and musicians and magicians and just strange people in general trying to earn money. Iz watched an old man, the color of bronze, bounce two large metal rods on a copper plate. They clanked and banged against the tray as she turned away to look at a man selling water. It was the sudden silence that made her look back at the metal rod man.

He was inches from her face, with the tray balanced on his head and the rods in his hands. With one swift move he shoved them up his nose, one up each nostril, then began a dull clunking sound as he bumped them together inside his head. Iz screamed, but no one heard her but the bead.

"You have seen nothing yet," said the bead. "Look at the big group behind you."

Both afraid not to and afraid to look, Iz turned. There were at least 20 women watching a man with a large basket and a flute. He sat upon the ground and lifted the lid off his basket. In the expectant quiet he started blowing on his flute, a slow, mesmerizing tune. Slowly a cobra's head appeared from inside the basket. It looked like it was in a trance as it swayed back and forth, constantly rising higher and higher out of the basket. The crowd watched captivated, especially the group of women at the back.

They were all dressed in long black robes, with black veils hiding all but their eyes. Although their expressions were hidden their tension was obvious in how close together they stood and grabbed each other's hands. They were so focused on the rising snake that none were aware of the man with a similar basket lurking behind them. Izdihar felt nervous just watching him, not sure what he was going to do. All she did know was that she hated snakes, had even lost a friend to a cobra bite at home.

She screamed, "Watch Out!" but once again it was like her words were swept away by a powerful *haboob* wind, and no one heard her. The screams of the woman though, caught everyone's attention. The man that Iz had worried about had walked up behind her and sat his basket down. He reached in and pulled out a cobra, which he dropped around the woman's neck. Her screams rang back and forth across the wide plaza, as she stood frozen, the snake dangling across her shoulders. Her eyes were wide open in the slit of her veil, and her screaming was painful to hear.

Her friend had dropped her hand and ran with the rest of the people as they scattered like ants fleeing water.

The snake began to slither across her shoulders, toward the ground, its tongue flicking wildly all the while. The man stepped forward and grasped the black cobra behind its head. The woman fainted as he pulled the rest of the snake off her.

"Why did he do that?" asked Izdihar. She was frantic and wanted to go home right then, but the bead tried to calm her. "Are we invisible? Did the man with the bars up his nose see me? Or was that coincidence? One thing is certain, no one heard my warning scream."

"*Calmetevi, calmetevi,*" shushed the bead. Be calm, be calm. "That snake man was looking for business. Now because of him there will be no business for anyone. I think we need to get on with this journey, so let's jump to N'Dar, not the proudest time of my life, but still in my youth."

Shameful Times

Izdihar smelled it before she saw it. The stench was strong and covered every other smell in the market. It was no great surprise, for hanging off hooks and over crossbeams, off shoulders and off donkeys were long strings of smelly dried fish.

"I have a question for you," she said to the bead. "How did you ever end up here?"

"Oh yes, another good question. It came as a shock, let me tell you my Iz. For more than 30 years I was pampered by the family of Sheik Abdul. I was passed from father to son; eventually the boy who served the tea, Mohammed, was my owner. They all spent hours appreciating my beauty and showing me off to their friends. And then, horrors of all horrors, the grandson betrayed me when he traded me to that woman there.

"My new owner was *Madame* N'Dour. She sold fish in the market during the day, and she was a juju *gri-gri* woman whenever anyone needed her services. The *juju*, you know it?"

Iz nodded her head yes, thinking of all the amulets and *gri-gri* pouches people used back home to protect themselves from sickness and curses. It occurred to her things hadn't changed much in the last few centuries. Even the fierce bargaining was the way of life in her village, with as much enthusiasm as Luigi's and *Signor* Castelli's and Sheik Abdul's. Only a fool would ever pay the first price asked. And people still believe and use black magic, she thought.

Izdihar looked around the market, where activity was bustling. There were the same stalls as at home, of fruit, and vegetables, and animal parts. Piles of live flapping fish caught her eye. "That is a new sight," she told the bead.

"Believe me, it is only the first of many new sights," replied the bead.

It didn't take long for a much bigger difference to register on Iz – women vendors were set up all throughout the market. Also, the majority of shoppers were women. They were shouting and laughing and carrying-on like Sudanese women at a closed women's party in her village near En Nahib. But here, in this place, all the women had their faces showing, and their shoulders exposed. Not one wore an over-cloth like Izdihar's *towb*.

"Do the men respect these women?" Iz asked the bead.

"What a question! Not the right... but an interesting

one. What makes you ask the question?"

"At home women cover their faces from time to time, and always cover their bodies. No shoulders showing, or legs, or sometimes, even hands. Where is their modesty? Men do not respect women who show their skin."

"Oh Iz, please do not be snobby. Different people have different ways, and they may have the same question about you, if they could see you wrapped up so tightly. I realize just now that this trip is the first step for you outside the Muslim world. Be like me, the rare and beautiful bead, and enjoy the differences."

The bead was silent for a moment, and then said in a very low voice, "This place, Iz, is *tritissimo*. Can you feel the sadness? For me it is a most shameful place. I have to admit, this is the only place I did not enjoy in my long and varied life. Can you feel it? It's a sad, shameful place."

Iz was still surveying the scene before her when she figured out exactly what the bead was talking about. She wasn't absolutely sure who they were at first, but then the emptiness in their eyes spoke loudly. There were men and women, chained together at the ankles, being marched through the market like a herd of sheep. Their chains clanked and they left blood along the way from the open sores on their feet and legs.

The bead could feel her sadness and said, "You're right, a slave market - the very lowest point of my life."

"Where are we?" she asked, finally looking away from the wretched people, tears glistening in her eyes. "Oh my God," she said aloud. "The girl I met at the well is a slave, isn't she? Her sadness feels just like these poor people." Iz tried to shake away the thought that Sudan still had slaves, captured Dinkas and Nuers from the south, where a war raged. For more than 20 years Muslims from the north and Christians and animists of the south had fought. "In my own village, in my own time, a slave lives?" Closing her eyes and giving her head a small shake, she asked again, "So, where are we?"

"It was N'Dar, the first time I was here. In your year of 2020 it is called Saint Louis, Senegal. It is only a small island in the Senegal River, but a major market for mankind's worst greed, selling human beings."

"But how did you get here? Did someone trade you for slaves?"

"Now that is an insulting, a _very_ insulting question. No and never has the world's most magnificent chevron been a bead of slavery! Chevrons have never been traded for slaves. Not ever!"

"Calm down," Iz said, rolling the bead softly between her palms. "*Malesh*. Really, I am sorry. I take the question back. But how did you get here?"

"I was betrayed by the grandson of Sheik Abdul, Sheik Mohammed. We came here for ivory, for he sold that as well as the gold. He got very ill and could not get better. So, while on death's doorstep he traded me to that woman, *Madame* N'Dour, so she could call on the gods for him for a cure.

"This woman, she had no appreciation for my beauty. She got me and wrapped me in a rag with other beads and coins and little *juju* packages, then stuffed us all into her waistline, under her long cloth skirt. It was worse than the three shirts of *Signor* Castelli. Only one layer of cloth cinched into the sweaty rolled waistline of her cloth wrap. That my colors are as strong as the day Luigi made me proves my very highest quality."

Iz rolled her eyes.

"Not one time did she show me off to her friends, or just take me out to admire my fineness. *Mai!*" Never!

Iz had to laugh, for the bead was clearly distressed. She bounced it in her palm, and the bead shouted, "STOP! If

52

you even drop me, lose contact with me for less than the time the sneeze takes, you will be lost forever. You will never get home again. So please, be careful and hold me tight. The responsibility of returning you to your home is getting to me."

Shaken by the bead's news, Iz went and sat next to a man resting against an old tree trunk lying on the ground. She rolled the bead again between her palms, and said, "Maybe I should wear you. That way I won't have such a huge responsibility either. If I fall asleep and drop you, then it is my fault that I never get home."

"*Esattamente!*" said the bead. Exactly! "Just slide me onto the bangle on your wrist, and then we shall always be connected. Believe me, this is the last place you want to get stuck."

Iz gently removed the silver bangle from her arm. She had never taken her bracelet off. Izdihar's mother had given it to her the day she turned ten. Her mother had received it on her 10th birthday too, passed all the way down from her grandmother's mother, always to the first-born daughter. Iz took the bead and slid it over one end of her bracelet. She moved the beautiful chevron toward the center, until it fit too tightly to move any further. Slowly, she forced the bangle back onto her slender wrist. It felt secure. She held her arm out, twisting it right and left, admiring the look of the chevron on her dark brown arm.

"This is beautiful," she said. "I wish you could look in a mirror, but I don't see one anywhere."

"And you won't see any mirror, until the year 1865. But look, look, *Madame* N'Dour has a customer."

Sheik Mohammed limped up to the woman. He was leaning on the shoulders of his oldest son and his man servant, his skin a pale version of his normal color. Sweat dripped from his brow, and he suddenly bent double in what looked like deep pain. He grabbed his stomach and dropped slowly to the ground. His moans carried loudly to where Iz sat.

"Maybe betrayed is too strong a word," said the bead as they watched the man writhe in pain. "Maybe desperate is the right word."

"I agree with you about that. What's wrong with him?" Iz asked.

"The bad belly. The kind that can kill you."

"Did he die?" she asked.

"The questions, they never stop, and they are never the right one. Just lean back and watch and see for yourself."

"*Salaam Aleikoum*," squeaked the sheik to the dried fish seller.

"*Na nga def.*" Hello, replied the woman in Wolof, each of them talking in their own language. She bent over and placed her hand on his arm, flinching back as she felt the heat of his body.

"Listen to this," said the bead. "He understands her language, Wolof, but doesn't speak it. And she is the same with the Arabic. They each talk in their own language and understand the other, just like the sheik's grandfather and the *signor*."

"I need help," said the sick sheik. "They tell me you can cure even the worst illness."

"I can give you help, but it will be expensive. Not just everyone can call the gods and have them answer," the woman boasted.

She eyed the quality of his gown, made from a beautiful shiny light green cloth. The embroidery was four different colors and covered nearly the front of his robe down to his waist. He wore a thick gold chain on his left arm, and the prayer beads wrapped around his other wrist were of the finest ebony. The woman took all this into account before she said, "I am sorry *sir*, but not even sacrificing 10 goats will be enough to save a man as sick as you."

"I will give you my greatest treasure, if you can only stop the pain."

"Here it comes," said the bead, "the most depressing moment in my life."

The sheik reached deep into his pocket as he lay on his side and brought out the softest of worn leather pouches. He opened it between the cramps that made him groan and brought out the bead. With effort he said, "This madame, is the finest of beads. When you cure me, my son will buy it back from you for 50 goats. I have not the goats now, but I do have *la malattia*, and need the cure now." And with that he completely collapsed.

The woman took the bead from his limp hand and looked at from all sides. It was beautiful, no doubt about that, but not worth 50 goats, she thought, maybe 30 at the most. It would be a good deal for her, she thought. Quickly she said, "Good. Let's go to my home."

The man was breathing in short little gasps, and it was clear that he wasn't going anywhere on his own. *Madame* N'Dour called four young men over. She pointed to them as she said to Sheik Mohammed's son, "Pay these boys, and they will carry the sick man to my house." Then she turned to the boys and told the oldest to run and get her hammock. "And don't forget the sticks," she called out as he left.

The young man quickly returned with two thick sticks, kind of crooked but very smooth, and a soft, woven hammock. They slung the hammock over a stick in front and the other in back, then the four placed the sheik onto the flattened cloth lying on the ground. With one even motion they stood together, lifting the hammock into the air. The one who had gone for the hammock let loose a shrill whistle through a wide gap in his front teeth and a path cleared before them.

The *madame*, turning over her dried fish to another woman sitting nearby, swung into the procession that carried the terribly ill man through the market. Iz rushed to keep up, for the very last thing she wanted to do was get lost in this wretched place. The going was quick until they ran into a long line of chained slaves. The tethered people couldn't move fast with their shackles, so the woman made the line stop, and spread as widely as they could between their chains. The boys carrying the sick sheik wormed their way through the line, none of them looking at the people they passed through.

It was the saddest thing Iz had ever seen. As fearful as she had been about getting left behind, she was now determined, invisible or not, to let the line of miserable humans pass. She just could not step between them as if they did not exist. Stressed by the sights she pleaded with the bead, "Please, can we leave this horrible place? Right now?"

"Just wait," said the bead. "Soon you will see something like you never have seen before."

Let's Go!

They finally arrived at the woman's hut, a little lopsided mud building with ears of corn drying on the rooftop. She scattered all the chickens that were pecking around her compound and stopped to pat a baby crying on her youngest daughter's hip. She pointed to a spot on the ground and told the boys, "Stand here. Do not put him down yet."

Madame N'Dour swept into her hut, then came backing out with the largest gourd Iz had ever seen. It could easily hold two serving platters at home, she thought. The woman took the baby and gave her daughter the gourd. The girl didn't even wait for instructions. Iz watched as she took the gourd to the well and filled it with water. She carefully carried it back to her mother, where a space had been cleaned for her to set it down. It balanced perfectly, like a giant tub, as the young girl took back the baby and went into the hut.

Madame N'Dour followed her into the hut, and this time brought out a smaller half gourd, decorated with a strand of cowry shells loosely attached to it. As she floated it upside down in the waiting gourd of water she started shouting, "Daughter, come now please."

A young woman, with a breast hanging out of her top came out of the hut with the same baby, greedily sucking down her mother's milk.

Izdihar couldn't help herself, gasping, "They even nurse in public!"

"It's just natural my dear," sang the bead. "But get ready for something super-natural soon."

"Yes mother?" asked the young woman un-enthusiastically as she shifted her baby.

"Bring your sticks and start playing. We need to call for help and when the women at home hear the beating of gourds they will come." With that she went into the hut, totally ignoring the four young men growing tired of holding the limp man in the hammock.

"Mother," shouted the oldest hammock-bearer, but she just waved her arm at him and went into her hut. The young mother passed her baby to another woman, then sat behind the smaller gourd floating in the larger gourd filled with water. She loosened her shoulders with an elaborate shrug, then began striking a loud beat — clack-clack, clack-clack. Women started to flow into the little compound, wearing more colors than the rainbow has, some clapping with the beat.

"How long does this last?" Iz asked with her hands over her ears. "I have a very bad feeling for this place and for this woman."

"It has not even begun yet," said the bead as two men with large wooden *balafones* hanging off of rope shoulder straps entered the compound. They sat next to the daughter, pounding on the gourd. "It sounds like someone hitting metal with metal," Iz yelled.

"Relax," said the bead.

As soon as the men sat the deep tones of the *balafones* filled the air, taking the edge off the gourd in the water with the clacking cowry shells. The young woman played faster, and the wooden xylophones kept up. The men were playing the thick wooden keys with heavy, carefully carved sticks. The sound was building just as *Madame* N'Dour made her entry.

She had changed into a deep, blood red gown and head tie decorated with gold embroidery. She looked nothing like the morning's fish seller. Iz sat staring at the regal woman that emerged from the hut. She stood taller than before and looked younger. She showed the tired carriers where to lay the hammock inside the circle that all the women had formed. With all eyes on her, she moved into the center of the circle.

The banging and the *balafones* stopped dead.

Madame looked once at the nearly unconscious Sheik Mohammed, then stood in front of him, facing the musicians. It started with a very slow repetitive beat - clack, clack, clack, pause, clack, clack, clack. With her eyes straight ahead, and a look of pure concentration on her face, the woman started a slow backstroke with her arms. The circles became bigger, and the beat increased.

Keeping up with the growing beat her arms flailed around in a wide, frenetic backstroke. Iz grabbed the bead on her wrist as she watched the woman's face change before her eyes.

"Spare me," cried the bead. "Let go! Maybe we need another place for me."

Iz dropped her hand and suddenly found her foot tapping to the ever-increasing, ear-splitting clacking beat. The woman's flailing arms slowly wound down to hang at her sides as all expression left her face. It reminded Iz of the old chalkboard at her school being wiped clean. She looked empty.

"She has reached the first stage of trance," said the

bead.

Madame N'Dour didn't stay still for more than a heartbeat when she started moving her head in slow circles on her totally limp neck. Like before, the gourd and *balafones* started a slow beat, and it was hard to tell if she drove the beat or the beat drove her, as her head wound round in a tight circle. Her neck and head fought to command the beat.

"Now this is truly the deep trance," said the bead.

She moved back into the middle of the circle, kicking up little blips of dust as she stamped her feet on the hard rocky ground. Iz felt her chin drop as she watched *Madame* N'Dour fall to the ground. Her body jerked in little spasms, and all the women rushed forward to pick her up. She shook with a big twitch, then stood and began shouting. Her head was thrust back, and she spoke to the sky in an insistent, monotone shout, in a language Iz was sure no one could understand. The instruments stopped as if she was waiting for an answer, then began again slowly. As she spoke women rushed up and rubbed her arms, hoping for contact with the powers she had reached.

Many women were dancing themselves into stupors or collapsed heaps looking just like the Whirling Dervishes Iz had seen in Sudan. That thought was replaced by panic when the bead suddenly screamed, "We must leave! *Immediatemente!*

Just then the *gri-gri* woman turned and stared right where Iz was standing.

"I thought we are invisible," cried Iz. "She's glaring right at me!"

"Let's go! Whoever she is talking to can see us, and so can she. Hang on!"

Bella

"Open your eyes," said the bead.

"The desert!" yelled Izdihar with delight. "I hope it's not Sudan," she said looking around her. It was strange, but she suddenly decided not to worry about her family anymore. She was sure that she was already in such deep trouble at home that what did another century or two matter? And she was definitely having the best time of her young, usually solitary life, and didn't want it to end yet.

"*Bella!*" she said.

"You can only mean me," answered the modest bead.

"Yes you. That's the name I've just given you, for giving me this trip, and also for your beauty." Looking around she added, "And for bringing me here, far from the terrible place and scary woman."

The bead sniffed a bit then said, "What a wonderful name. And so appropriate. Are you sure the name *Molta Bella* is not better? The name my artistic maker Luigi first gave me. Very beautiful seems much more appropriate."

"How about if I just call you *Molta?*" asked Iz.

"No no no! Bella will be just fine. Now start again, call my name."

"Bella," called Izdihar, "where are we and when are we? And how did we get here? And what happened to *Madame* N'Dour? And what about Sheik Mohammed? Did she cure him?"

"Stop," said Bella. "One question at a time. I'm old don't forget, over 200 years. Please, take the time to ask your endless questions one by one. We have a long walk ahead of us."

Iz looked at the swinging rhythm of the large cattle herd, 12 young herdsmen, and one older man. She asked as casually as possible, "So, where are we?"

"A good question. I am most happy to say that we are far from the miserable N'Dar, Senegal, and getting close to the Niger River, in Mali, on the southern stretches of the Sahara Desert. And before you ask the second question, we are five years later."

"And the sheik?"

"He didn't make it. A very large woman collapsed on him, and that was more than the poor man could withstand. His son was so upset he left without buying the goats to buy back my beautiful own self, the chevron, and *Madame* N'Dour was not happy. Never before has someone died in her compound. Or not paid her in full."

"So, she traded you to these cow herders for????"

"For four powerful amulets. And I was not traded to cow herders, but to the man over there. And so here we are, with the Fulani of Mali, who have been away from their families for six months, and one lone Hausa man who has been gone longer. He is the most important one here — my new owner — the smart, the wisdomful, a humble holy man from Niger, Marabout Karim. It's wonderful, so magnificent to breathe fresh air again. *Al Hamdillilai!*"

"Oh Bella, it's true. Praise Allah! We are out in the open, just like my home. The crowds and the hustle and the noise are gone." She twirled with her arms outstretched, face turned toward the late afternoon sun. Looking ahead and then back over her shoulder she asked, "How many cows are there?"

The herd stretched on and on, each cow walking at its own gait, some followed by young calves. It was a wide sea of motion on the desert savannah landscape. Two donkeys carried large, bulging bundles, sticking far out beyond their bellies. She surprised herself when she added, "And such handsome herders!"

Eleven of the young men walked along the outskirts of the herd, escaping the growing dust cloud that built behind them. They wore long cotton gowns with trousers, covered in dust. Ten of the herders wore shepherd's hats, no two alike, and two wore turbans. The marabout wore a gown of brown and gold, with a tight little prayer cap of mixed colors on his head.

"My but these herders are handsome," gushed Iz. She immediately clapped her hand over her mouth, embarrassed by her outburst.

The youngest herder, closer to Izdihar's age than the others, followed the herd, his mouth and nose covered by the end of his turban. He walked along casually, collecting any dung left by an animal, for the night's cooking fires. Iz thought about just that afternoon, in her real life, doing the same work, nearly 200 years later. How can we still be doing the same things, she wondered? Haven't we made any progress? The answers she could think of were disappointing, especially when she thought of the young slave girl in her village, so she went back to looking around.

As Iz gazed at the group she asked, "Where do they live? And why have they been gone so long?" Almost reluctantly she added, "Have we been gone a long time?"

"Oh, my Iz, always questions and more questions, and never the right one. Just look around you, you who loves the desert. There is almost a kind of beauty in this place." Hastily Bella added, "But not beauty to compare to my own, is that not so?"

Izdihar looked around, ignoring Bella's plea for a compliment. The men, walking tall, called to one another, joking, and laughing as they walked along. "They look young, especially the dung collector." Then focusing on Karim, she said, "The holy man walks alone, his prayer beads moving through his fingers as if they are alive." He reminded her of her father, always busy with his prayer beads.

Huge silent dunes, of sharp angles and round edges, filled the horizon far off in the distance. Shadows cast by the sinking sun left one dune divided in half by a blanket of shadow covering one side. Iz sucked in her breath at the beauty of it all. Not a drop of water in sight, or the silhouette of a well as far as she could see.

She shook herself, and then said, "How did we get here? What did you pay for? Oh yes, the amulets. We also have amulets in Sudan."

"The ones the *juju* woman traded me for were little black and red leather pouches. Two were for the neck, and two for tying around the biceps. Each pouch has a verse of the Koran, chosen and copied by Marabout Karim."

"We have *marabouts* too, the religious learned men, and the same amulets," said an excited Iz. "What did she get? Powerful ones can be expensive."

"Iz, the expense was great, and my honor restored. Normally, an amulet to protect the person from death or disease, loss of fortune or a bad future cost at least one cow and a few smaller animals. So, four amulets from the most holy of Hausa men, *mama mia*! That means I am worth more than four cows!"

"But what about the amulets? We already know how rare and beautiful and modest you are," joked Iz.

"The first amulet was no surprise. She asked for protection from the sheik's family, something to prevent all bad against her, even stopping spears. The second was to protect her family, keep them together always. *Numero tre* was not so nice. It was to keep her healthy by sending illness onto anyone who may wish to harm her or her family.

"The fourth one the wise marabout refused to make, an awfully bad one indeed. She wanted it to make the fat woman who had fallen on the sheik, go crazy, turn her family against her, and force her to leave N'Dar."

The bead's voice dropped to nearly a whisper as it said, "The sheik dying in her compound, in the way he did, was such a disgrace for *Madame* N'Dour. To disgrace a woman with her powers is the greatest of mistakes. For me, the greatest of luck was her meeting Karim, and trading for four powerful amulets with the power of my beauty!"

"So, if he refused to make the wicked request, what was the fourth amulet for?"

With pride Bella said, "He made one for the baby that was in the compound, asking that if she desires, she learn the ways of her grandmother. A good wish, no?"

Izdihar nodded slowly, not sure that it was such a great idea, for didn't the grandmother practice *juju*? Thoughtfully she said, "I like that the baby's future depends on her choice. I wish that someone had made an amulet for me with that wish." Looking at the bead on her wrist she asked, "Do you see my future, since you see the past so clearly?"

Bella sighed and said, "Do you think that is the question that will get you home? Do you not remember that the right question is bigger than you, or your needs?"

"I know that," said Izdihar. "And I'm thinking about what it could be. All good questions take time, I now

71

know."

Bella then said, "No, I do not see the future, only the memories of my past. Oh, this was another wonderful time in my life, here with the Fulani herders and the wise Marabout Karim."

Iz looked around. The sun was on its downward arc, closer to the horizon than the heavens. The herder in front, a tall handsome young man with skin a coppery black, and a smile as white as the distant dunes, waved his arm in the air, signaling the others that here is where they would stop. When the young dung collector arrived with one of the donkeys, he quickly unlashed a large leather bag made from cowhide that hung off the animal's neck.

Squatting on the flat desert sand the boy first adjusted his turban. The cloth was 18 inches wide and 12 feet long. He easily re-wound it around his head, flicking the cloth over the lower half of his face into looser folds, hiding everything but his eyes. As he opened the bag, the other herders dropped to the ground around him. They greeted one another like they hadn't met for days.

The young herder opened the soft leather bag he had taken from the donkey. Saying, "Here Baka," he handed a small teapot like a child's toy to the tall young man waiting patiently beside him.

Baka tenderly wiped clean the already clean surface of the shiny green teapot before setting it on the ground. He piled cow dung into the base of a small, wire basket, then dropped a few coals from the bag on top of the dung. Next, he placed a flat stone on the ground and piled a few dried stalks of grass from the same bag. With a practiced motion he flicked a larger stone against the flat one until a spark jumped to life. He quickly dumped the baby flames onto the dung and charcoal, and once a bed of coals formed, he neatly tucked his teapot onto the heat.

"We might as well relax," said Bella, "for these tea ceremonies go on for a very long time."

Iz shook the dust from the front of her *towb* and asked, "May I ask them for some tea?"

"Oh, you could ask, but then you would stay here forever, for if you make contact it is forever. Per s*empre,* as they say. Forever!"

Iz thought of Fanta, and her parents. Did she really never want to see them again? Or bothersome Khalil? "I have a job," she suddenly announced to Bella. "If I can't stop my marriage, or be what I want when I grow up, then I shall spend my life making sure the same does not happen to my little sister. She will be free to be whom and what she wants. Just like the prayer in the amulet Marabout Karim made for the little girl in Senegal so long ago."

"It's a big job," said the bead, "but one you will do well if you dedicate yourself."

Iz turned to take a better look around her. With a gasp she told Bella, "How did I not see these before?"

Bella snorted and said, "Because you were too, yes too busy my dear, admiring, and I quote you, 'the handsome herders!'"

Iz took off at a run, forgetting the long hours of walking she had already done that day.

Baobab Heaven

A giant smile spread across Iz's face, just like the growing shadows spilling across the savannah. Before her stood the largest collection of baobab trees she had ever seen.

"Those are the best gift God ever gave the poorest of men," said the bead. "You can eat its seeds, make tea with its flowers, cook stew with its leaves, and make rope or clothing from its bark."

Iz knew all of this already, being a girl of the stark Sudanese Sahel. But she let Bella talk so she could just gaze upon the magnificent beauty of the ancient trees. There were 17 majestic baobabs spread out before her, almost like a forest. Beyond the first 17 were many more silent silhouettes, almost too numerous to count.

Quietly, as if in awe, she walked up to the nearest tree. "Bella," she said, "we must measure her girth – for I am sure that this beauty is an old mother tree. Look at how huge she is." Spreading her arms as widely as she could around the trunk, Iz gave the great tree a giant hug. She checked the ground around its base for something to mark her starting point.

Stepping back to collect two stones the size of her fists, she held one in each hand. Spanning the giant trunk once again, she dropped each stone. One marked where she had begun and the other where her arm span had ended. Moving slowly around the tree, left hand meeting where the right hand had been, she counted, "*Sittasahar, saebae tashar, taemaentashar*". Sixteen, seventeen, eighteen.

"Eighteen arm spans. I wonder if anyone stores water inside?" This time she walked around the tree's trunk, but at a distance. Its bark, a mottled grey, held scars that showed animals and people had used the tree through the centuries. As she walked around, she kept her eye on the top of the trunk, where giant thick branches reached out, each sprouting into thinner and thinner twigs.

When Iz finished her circumnavigation of the tree, she lifted her arm to look at the bead. She couldn't help but notice how smooth and rich Bella looked against her skin, the color of the strongest tea.

Proudly she said, "We have a baobab tree at home that we use as a giant water gourd. My family has used and cared for our tree for generations. We store water that we collect during the short rainy season inside of her."

Patting the rough bark of the giant baobab she said,

"But this tree cannot be a giant gourd, for there is no door at the top." Running her hand along a series of deep ridges in the strong bark Izdihar muttered, "I think someone has used her for rope-making though."

Immediately Iz thought of her grandmother, who had taught her the baobab's secrets and gifts. With a shiver she said, "I thank Allah she is no longer with us. She would be worried sick about me. I guess that is, if anyone has noticed me missing."

Looking again at Bella, Iz said, "I know you said I needed a meaningful question to return home, so let me ask you one I once asked my grandmother. She did not have an answer for me, but maybe you will. Please don't laugh at me if it's the wrong question."

"You underestimate me my dear," replied the bead. "Even though I am proud of my beauty that does not grow dimmer with time, I have learned many things along the way. I must admit that I am a beautiful bead and a brilliant bead, for my knowledge is vast.

"Just think about all the things I know about the grandest tree in Africa — maybe the world. So, ask any serious question you have, and prepare for wisdom that matches my beauty. Do not forget, I have been owned by the holy man, Marabout Karim, and by a scholarly imam, but let's not get ahead of ourselves."

Iz straightened her shoulders and squeezed her eyes shut as she asked, "What is truth?"

"Humph," said Bella. "A very interesting question, and better than most of yours so far. Truth – yours or mine? I mean we all have our own truth, as Karim told the handsome herder one day. If we each live by our personal, main truth, that is what makes each of us the individuals we are."

Stopping for the shortest of breaths Bella continued, "My main truth is that I am beautiful and valuable, which permits me to bring pleasure to more people than I can count. That is my service to mankind."

Iz looked at the bead, then back at the giant baobab that needed 18 arm spans to be hugged. Without any prompting from Bella she said, "My truth must be that I don't know what it is yet."

"It was a very good question, whether you have the answer yet or not. Let us hope that with time these travels will lead you to the answer you seek," replied Bella. "And the question you need."

The Hausa Holy Man

Just then, the sweetest sound Izdihar had ever heard floated across the arid landscape. She looked over her shoulder at the Fulani nomads relaxing around the little teapot. Four men drank from the smallest of glasses as they listened to the man on the flute play a tribute to the cows that had walked the entire long, hot day.

"These people love their cows," said Bella. "They have led them to water and pasture, far from their family groups. Now they are taking them back again, to the swampy lands that will grow with the rains on the other side of the mighty Niger River."

"The cows can swim?" asked a surprised Izdihar.

The notes of the flute trickled up and down. One hefty bull, white with black spots like saddlebags across his back, shook its head with large pointed horns, swiveling it back and forth. In a sudden trot he headed out of the herd. Neither the man playing the flute, nor anyone else for that matter, panicked when the animal burst out of the herd. Instead, the flute man trilled three rapid high notes – tweet, tweet, tweet! As if running into a wall the bull stopped dead in his tracks, then turned and returned to the heart of the herd.

"Did you see that?" asked an excited Bella. "The beast knew the call for only him, saying stay! These people truly are one with their animals."

As Bella spoke the marabout took his prayer rug from the back of the donkey he had ridden part of the afternoon. He spread it on the hard-packed savannah floor, then knelt, facing east and Mecca. Izdihar caught her breath and said, "I thought he looked Muslim and now I know he surely is. Why does he pray alone?"

Bella answered promptly. "Because he is a Hausa holy man of Niger. His companions are Fulani, and though they may call on Allah in times of need, they are not necessarily strict practicers of the Islamic faith. They are nomads, with a dedication to family and herds and the balance of nature."

Suddenly another five cows started to move out of the herd. The flute man played a warning, but four cows kept moving. The youngest herder jumped to his feet and chased them back into the herd, his knob-headed herding stick waving in the air and his tongue clicking loudly. He ran in the hot dusty evening with as much energy as someone starting their day rather than someone on the edge of dusk.

Bella spoke with admiration as it said, "These Fulani are amongst the best of herders. Just look at this harsh environment, challenging and sort of ugly."

"It's not ugly!" snapped Izdihar. "It's beautiful. It looks just like my home – hard earth, scattered trees and scrub brush, and great dunes in the very far distance."

Bella carried on as if Iz hadn't interrupted. "These Fulani balance with nature like no other men. And they are smart, bringing along a marabout. Karim connects them to Allah, while they themselves connect to the spirits of their ancestors and Mother Nature."

Iz wasn't really listening. She was watching Marabout Karim follow the ritual of prayer, thinking of her father all the while. Her father was a devout but not fanatic Muslim and had often said that there are different degrees of Islam. He believed Allah was merciful, while there were others who thought Allah believed in war. Her father could never understand how some people could think that Allah would want someone killed in his name. He had told her mother more than once, "A religious war is the strangest concept on Allah's big earth."

As Iz watched the marabout say his prayers she felt in her heart that he was not a Muslim who believed in war.

Karim prayed, and the Fulani herdsmen went about their business. Two men pulled a large sack off one donkey. Baka adjusted his conical shepherd's hat made of leather and thick woven straw that provided a wide brim. He told his companion, "Let's wait until the marabout has finished his prayers so he can bless the *djenne* grass before we feed the cows. He will surely make it stronger, giving them the night sight they need to travel in the darkness."

"They travel at night?" Iz asked Bella.

"Yes, my dear, at night too. They are on their way home after six long months of heat and dust and one another for company. They are hurrying, for a great celebration will occur when they reach the southern bank of the river. You are fortunate, for I have only brought you on the last few days of the trek. To see these cattle cross the river is something I am sure you have never seen in the savannah you described to me."

Iz's jaw dropped. "How do these cows cross a river? Is it so shallow they just walk across? Or do they swim?"

"Wait and see," was all Bella said.

"So why is the marabout with them if they are Fulani herdsmen and he is a Hausa holy man?"

"After making the four pouches for the juju woman of

N'Dar he spent four more years, studying with a marabout in a place called Casamance. When he heard that the Fulani were ready to start their trek back across the wide-open spaces, to Mali, and the land near his home in Niger, he knew it was time for him to go home.

"He found a young man and paid him to take him to a group to join." Bella stopped talking just as the marabout arose from his prayers.

Fulani Magic

When Karim had folded his mat and tied it back onto the donkey, the taller Fulani, Baka, who had waited patiently for him called out respectfully, "Father, please come bless our *djenne* grass that gives us and our cows strong sight at night."

The marabout walked over to the large sack they were holding. He took a fistful of the dried grass stalks from the bag. Turning once again toward Mecca he held the grass in his outstretched arm, whispering words just he could hear. With a solemn face he touched the bundle to his heart, one, two, three times. He then stuck the blessed blades of grass back into the center of the bag.

"You see, he is working for his passage with the group. He brings Allah to the journey and they bring food and tea and companionship." As an afterthought Bella added, "And I bring the beauty."

It was as if Karim had heard Bella, for in that moment he reached into the deep pocket in his gown and brought out the bead. He rolled it between his palms as he watched the men give each cow some of the night vision grass.

Once all the herders and Karim had drunk three glasses

of tea, the flute man started playing, and all the resting cows rose to their feet again. As the cows stood, so did all the young men. Each one carried a long, slender stick with a knobby head. Casually they fanned out around the herd, in pairs or alone. Except for the lowing of the cows and the floating flute notes, the night was quiet. Each man walked with a steady pace, moving the cows east and south, toward the mighty Niger River.

Izdihar fell into the same pace. She looked at the bead and said, "It's good I'm not real here, because in real life I could never, no not ever, walk all day in the pounding sun and intense heat, and then continue walking toward dawn."

The night was cool, with the temperature dropping many degrees when the sun dropped beyond the horizon. "It makes sense to walk at night," Iz said.

"Especially to them, because they are walking toward family life. They have not seen family or friends, or even girls, for six long months. They are very determined young men right now. At this rate we will be at the river's edge tomorrow afternoon, and then you will see a spectacle not to be believed."

As the herd wandered past, the marabout stood to the side saying again and again, "*Al Hamdillilai, Allah!*" blessing the twelve herdsmen and more than 100 cows. Karim fell into step with Baka when he drew near. The handsome young man said, "You are a strong man Father, for you never complain of travel all day and then travel all through the night."

Karim touched the young man's arm and said, "I am as eager as you to return to family and friends." Once again, he pulled the bead from his pocket, rolling it between his palms. "It's been five rainy seasons since I have seen my home."

The tall herder pointed at Karim's hands and asked, "What have you got there?

A sudden chortle filled the air as Bella yelled in glee, "It's me! Beautiful me!"

Karim held the bead between thumb and forefinger, just like Luigi and Signor Castelli, Sheik Abdul, and Izdihar. Its shape and smoothness seemed to glow in the growing moonlight.

Bella shrieked again, "Listen to this!"

Karim handed the bead to the young Fulani and said, "This is the best payment I have ever received. Its beauty is rare..."

"Rare — did you hear that? Rare is only a fraction of my

beauty!" cried Bella.

Iz shook her wrist with impatience. "Please be quiet. Where is all the wisdom and brilliance you were bragging of earlier?"

Karim took the bead back from Baka, and again rolled it between his worn palms. "I hope this bead will buy me a bride, for it is definitely a beautiful dowry gift. But first I must get to Niger, my homeland. I am from a small village on the very river we are going to cross. With any luck, I will find transport on the river, and not have to walk home."

As an afterthought, he added, "And with better luck I will not have to part with this fine bead for transport, as it is time for me to marry a Hausa woman who will bless me with many children." Shaking his head from side to side he said, "I hope it doesn't take me as long to reach home as it did to get to Senegal, and back again this far."

Baka patted his shoulder and said, "We will help you find transport when we reach the south bank, for many will be gathered there." Karim dropped his head in a quick bow, an emotional sign that he appreciated Baka's offer.

And so, they traveled through the night, each lost in his own thoughts. Izdihar walked at a pace with the slowest cows, thinking as she went. "Bella," she said in the coldest moment of the day or night, just before the arrival of the dawn. "If I ask you another question that I've asked my father but still have no answer for, will the Brilliant Bella or the Beautiful Bella answer?"

"I guess it depends on the question. If it is one that involves wisdom, which I have, then that is who will answer. And if it is a me, me, me question, which you have been known to ask, then it will be a me, me, me answer."

"To me that is fair. Oh, there's that word."

"Just ask, *Cara Mia*, and I shall do my best to answer."

"Why is there war? Why can't life just be like this, peaceful with people of different tribes and religions getting along?"

"Well, that is quite a question. What makes you ask it?"

"I have been thinking about it since watching the marabout pray and the others not joining him - but respecting his right to do so amongst them. It made me think of the war in my country. We don't see it, except for the poor Dinka girl that I now realize is a slave and a victim of that war. But my country has been warring with its own countrymen since before I was born. About religion mainly if I understand it correctly.

"I wish we lived now, in this moment, where peace

exists, and people like one another no matter where they come from or what they believe."

"Oh, my dear, I have bad news for you. War has been around longer than even me. In fact, when we finish this idyllic stroll, we will cross Mali and Niger, to Nigeria, where war rules for many of the years we are there. What makes it so strange is that it is a war of religion, and the brethren of these peaceful Fulani are some of the biggest armies, eager to force Islam on all who are not followers.

"I know, I called them casual Muslims not so long ago. But some who are more settled have taken the faith and have taken it upon themselves to spread the word. My dear, I suggest that we live in this moment, while we can, for something wonderful will happen this evening. Something I call Fulani magic."

River Madness

The dawn brought a red sun, peeking up over the giant baobabs scattered on the landscape before them. The trees were fewer, but just as grand as the one Iz had hugged, was it really only the night before? "Bella, please don't get angry, but I hope we haven't been gone long enough for my family to notice. For worry they will if I don't get home before the time for bed."

Bella remained silent, which worried Iz worse than a snappy answer. "I didn't ask it as a question. And If I had, it was bigger than just me," she almost whined. "It was about my parents. They will worry so."

"I'm sure your family is fine."

"But just think Bella. We have been to Italy, Morocco, and Senegal. All places on my beautiful map. And now we have walked across the width of West Africa, from the Atlantic Ocean to the Sahara toward the shores of the big river you talk about. Can it really all have been done in only hours?"

"Please," said the bead. "Do you not realize yet how good this trip is for you? We are not just exploring a continent, but also discovering your future. And the biggest challenge of all – we're hoping to open your mind, so you know different isn't bad – it's just different."

Iz looked at her wrist and told the bead, "Oh Bella, please do not doubt that this trip has taught me much. And although I worry that I have been gone too long, I also worry that the right question may not come."

Rubbing the bead with the pad of her thumb she said, "This has been the best thing to ever happen to me. Not only have I seen all these places, but I have also thought about things important to more than just me."

"Good," said Bella, "for I can see changes in you. The important thing though, is that you see them too, and I think you do. Now, can we just enjoy this time right now?"

Looking up, Iz watched the herd, its dust trail turning a faded red in the growing sunlight cast by a rising, fire-red sun. Iz could feel the excitement building as the handsome young herders gleefully called to one another in the already growing heat.

"Listen to them Iz. They are calling out the names of girls left behind, who will be young women just like they are now the young men of their group. Tomorrow they shall meet again, each eager to impress the other."

Even with the growing heat and the endless hours of

walking, the men and cows continued on. The sun climbed in the sky and the hard-packed earth seemed to have no end in sight. Iz had fallen into a walking stupor when she suddenly heard shouts. She looked up in time to see two running figures, shimmering in the wavy heat that hugged the horizon. "Are they a mirage?" she asked. She knew they weren't when Baka and another herdsman ran toward the approaching silhouettes.

The cows began to moo with much more force than before. They also broke into a run, as if following Baka's lead. The eleven remaining herders quickly followed, running, and jumping, and crying out greetings. Marabout Karim bounced on the donkey he rode as it trotted to keep up with the racing animals.

"They can smell it," cried Bella. "Water! These boys coming to greet us are from the river, where they have been waiting for the sight of our great dust cloud to let them know the cattle are returning. As well as their friends and brothers."

The meeting was joyous. Hugs and hand slaps, whoops, and laughter, filled the air. Baka pointed back at the herd, obviously proud of all the cows and calves that were on their way to the water. As the cows reached the young men, they all broke out into a full run, toward Allah's greatest gift, ample water after a long and dry trip.

"*Mama mia,*" said Bella. "We are in for a wonderful time."

Iz stopped in her tracks. Before her stood a wide brown liquid ribbon, moving quickly. Unlike the ocean she had been on, this water was bordered on both sides, by land that was dried and hard. Land that looked like it hadn't seen water in years, although it spilled west and east, south and north, from the river. Iz had never seen the Nile River, so seeing the Niger was heart stopping. "It's beautiful," she whispered. "And it looks so powerful. Look how swiftly it moves."

"Do you see why it is called The Strong Brown God?" asked Bella.

"Indeed," was all she said as she stood and watched.

The bank of the river wasn't too steep, and the cows poured down it, to drink their fill from the swiftly moving brown water. Three small boats were tied to the bank, where two more young men awaited the cows and herders. The two whooped when they saw their friends.

The young greeters rushed down the bank and jumped into the empty canoe. They couldn't wait to tell all the others waiting on the far side of their friends' arrival. With one young man standing in front, and the other on the stern of the small wooden boat, they dipped their paddles into the brown water. Tipping and wobbling, the canoe rushed down the center of the river, at an angle toward the other bank, which looked far away to Iz.

Their voices were raised in joy as the boat was swept around a bend, rapidly moving out of sight. Baka looked at the herders, as if to say, "Do you see what we are in for — with our cows?"

Almost as an answer an admiring Bella said, "River madness."

A Wise Leader

Activity filled the camp. The waiting young men had food for the cows, which they spread on the ground. The cows moved from water to sustenance, eager for the fresh grass stalks after quenching their great thirst. The young men drank tea and unpacked a big bag hanging off one of the donkeys. Izdihar marveled at the collection of beautiful clean robes and cloths pulled from the bag. There were also little pots of dried color, and brushes made from cow's tail.

Baka was the first to enter the water, up to his knees, washing the grit and sweat of the six-month-long march to grazing, and back. "I'm sure he's remembering that when they had crossed this same river in June, the cattle had walked sedately across the shallows of the shrunken Niger," Bella told Izdihar. The rushing river in December shared no resemblance to the exposed river bed of the dry season in June. Then it had been large puddles scattered on the river bottom.

"Does the herder know where this river starts?" asked Iz. "I know that our great Nile is the joining of the Blue Nile from our neighbor Ethiopia, and the White Nile, which comes from Uganda. They meet in Khartoum, where I hope to study one day."

"Baka has no idea where the river starts, but I know because of the scholar who owns me next. This river, so tame in dryness and strong in wetness, actually begins in three small pools in the Futa Jalon area of Guinea. Baka only knows that when the rains start at the mouth, the river fills and life is easy for a time, for both man and beast."

They watched as Baka rubbed the grit from his skin with mud from the bank, a muddy mess thanks to the cows' hooves that had just been there. He gazed down river, as if gauging the challenge that still awaited them. Successfully taking the herd to pasture and back could not be celebrated until the final hurdle had been completed – getting the cattle safely across the rapidly flowing Niger River.

The youngest herder joined Baka at the water's edge. He was soon followed by all the rest of the herders, while Marabout Karim spread his prayer rug and bowed to the east. Iz was certain he was thanking Allah for their safe arrival and praying for a successful crossing.

The afternoon was like a party. The men sat around, bragging about who would look the best for the young women that awaited them on the other side. Each had special clothes he had carried just for this event. Colors sprouted on the bank like the arrival of a bunch of butterflies. The flute man filled the air with joyous notes, congratulating the cows on their journey so far, and urging them to braveness and calmness for the challenge still to come.

"We shall start crossing at first light," said Baka as he poured a small amount of water into a pot holding blue powder. He stirred it with a cow hair brush, making a thick paste. As he talked, he painted a large blue circle around the eye of his favorite bull. Iz noticed it was the bull that had broken out of the herd just the night before.

Baka's voice was calm but excited as he said, "We will start across the river with the two strongest bulls. This will give the others the confidence they need to enter the water. We will leave three other bulls for the other groups, to encourage the reluctant ones to get into the water."

All the young men nodded their heads in agreement. One was painting a red diamond on his bull's head, and another a pyramid shape of green on his pet. The others rested in the late afternoon sunlight, a well-deserved break after the intense last few days of almost continuous walking. "We shall sleep well tonight," said the youngest herder proudly.

Baka looked at him with a bright smile, and made the boy glow when he said, "You have done well, younger brother. Some thought you were too young to make this trip, but you have proved them wrong. Sleep tonight, for the dawn brings the biggest challenge yet. Don't forget, you will be one of the herders in the water, so we need you strong and ready. I hope that this is not a bad judgment on my part. What do you think?"

Iz watched as the boy puffed his chest out with more confidence than she was sure he felt. "I shall succeed," he said.

"After that accomplishment, you will really enjoy the celebration we have all been looking forward to since we left," Baka said, pushing over the turban wrapped loosely on the boy's head.

Just then Marabout Karim walked up. His prayer mat was tucked beneath his arm. He wore a beautiful gown of yellow and blue, and a smile that rivaled Baka's. "If I may," he said, "I would like to offer a special thanks for our journey so far. I would also like to offer a grateful thanks to Allah for your companionship and company on a trip I could never have made alone."

Baka stood and said, "Please Father, let us join you in this prayer. May we also ask for a safe journey tomorrow?"

"You see?" Bella said. "It's like I said before, they know to ask Allah for help in special times. You can be sure they will also be asking their ancestors for help in keeping the cattle afloat during the crossing."

The marabout spread his prayer rug on the ground, facing Mecca. The herders knelt around him. All faced east waiting for the heartfelt words of the holy man.

"I remember when you called them casual Muslims. It is clear to me that they don't often pray like us, for some do not touch their heads to the ground. Are you sure it is the Fulani who fight for Islam?" Iz asked.

"Absolutely," replied Bella. "But what do you think, shall we not also join in the prayer, for don't forget, we must also cross this raging river."

Iz noticed the youngest herder. His face was a conflict of joy and fright, as he shut his eyes in a tight squint. Iz thought, "I am sure he is thinking about his swim to come. Please Allah, keep him safe."

Shortly after the prayers the night was filled with the lowing of contented cows and the snores of exhausted herders. Floating on the air, like the soft flute of nights before, was the sound of Marabout Karim's voice, talking to his prayer beads that swiftly moved in his right hand. Iz fell asleep in a moment she called in her mind, true peace.

The calmness that had sent Iz to sleep was replaced by a buzz of activity in the morning. Tea was prepared before the sun actually appeared, and the cattle were roused from their sleep. The flute man played with gusto like never before. Baka was giving out gentle commands. He pointed to two strong young men and said, "You will carry the donkeys across in that canoe, along with the baby cows, for they surely cannot swim. Abu, you have managed a canoe before, is that not so?"

Abu nodded yes. It was clear that relief swept across his and his companion's face as they knew for sure they would not be in the water. Baka looked at the youngest herder and said, "Little brother, stay close to me in the water. I have crossed before with the cows and if you feel fearful or too tired, I will help you." Then looking deep into his eyes, he told him, "But I know you will do well."

Turning to the marabout, Baka said, "Father, after one last blessing you shall ride with these six in the bigger canoe."

"Baka," said a young man, dressed in a gown of rich

purple, "let me change back into my tired clothes and swim with you, for there can never be too many in the water." The leader nodded with appreciation to the herder, and then said, "Marabout Karim, you shall ride with these five."

Another young herder stood and said, "I too shall go in the water. For why would the best swimmer of all ride, when he can escort his favorite bull by his side?"

His friend standing nearest called out, "I shall show you all who is the best water man. I know that all the girls waiting will see me as the finest too!"

"We will see about that," said the first.

"So that is three in the boat," said the marabout. Laughter erupted, breaking the growing tension as the moment of entry approached.

Iz watched Baka as he talked to the ones who would swim with him. "He's a wise leader," she told Bella. "Instead of telling everyone what to do he let them offer their services."

Bella replied, "If you can see that then you also will be a good leader."

Izdihar couldn't help but smile.

Just Different

The three young men who were riding with the marabout made final checks on their special gowns. The swimmers changed into their walking clothes, giving the paddler of the canoe the bundles of their celebration clothes to take to the other side. Suddenly all fell silent as the marabout softly cleared his throat. "*Allahu Akbar!*" he cried. God is great! "Allah most powerful, may you continue to protect and guide us as we face this final challenge. We place our trust and lives in your most merciful hands. *Allahu Akbar!*"

"*Bisimallah!*" responded the nervous but excited young herders. In the name of God!

Clapping his hands together, Baka said, "May the final challenge begin. We will go in groups of three herders, and as many cows as we can."

All the young men fanned out behind the cows. The mooing took on a loud, disgruntled tone as the first two bulls and 30 or more cows were herded toward the water. The bulls entered to drink, and were surprised when they were lightly struck with the knobby-headed herd sticks to keep moving forward. As their feet left the safety of the bottom their eyes bulged in shock. The ones following were also surprised, but they struggled to stay close to their leaders.

Not ten feet from the shoreline the swift current swept them downstream. Baka raced along in the current on the north side of the cows, nudging them toward the south bank as the water carried them along. It was important to have the first group on a good course, so those to come would follow roughly on the same route.

Izdihar sucked her breath in; amazed by the bravery it took to be the first into the water. She watched the young brother thrash about as his head went under for the first time. Baka swam his way, but the boy emerged and shook his head. He said something to Baka, who then turned and resumed his efforts to keep the herd moving across the river as they were swept downstream. The first herder to volunteer brought up the rear of the group, swinging his club toward any cow that faltered.

"Oh Bella, I am so happy that we shall cross in a pocket of the holy man. For although I loved the boat on the sea, with the wind and waves, to jump into this chaos I would find impossible to do." Her eyes shined as she watched the next bunch of cows slip down the well-worn mud path to the water. They mooed and bellowed as they slid down the muddy path. Each splashed into the water and was quickly driven off by the next three herders who had volunteered.

The final cow group, steered by the two who had bragged about their skills, was forced into the water. There was enough space between swimming herds to make sure that no cow overcame another, but also not too much distance for them to see the shortest route taken by the leaders. When all the cows were in the water the two canoes, carrying the donkeys, four calves and the men, took to the water. The marabout sat near the paddler in the back, watching the men in front stand as the boat tilted back and forth, side to side, as it caught the current.

"Thank God he is sitting," said a nervous Izdihar. She gazed at the herders, one dressed in a spotless white gown with matching pants, his head covered by his shepherd's hat. He was chanting loudly with his companions, one dressed in blue with a purple turban, and the other wearing a blue and white checked gown. He swung his herder's stick in time to the chant.

"Their voices give the ones in the water confidence," said Bella. "They didn't swim because they are afraid, for they have an important purpose also. They stayed out of the water to urge men and beasts across. Look, even the flute man is chanting, sending words of encouragement to his friends."

Before Baka's group of cows reached the far shoreline, they heard shouts from the other bank. The young men that had met them the day before ran along the high bank, followed by a crowd of Fulani, young and old, there to welcome the herders home.

Beautiful young Fulani women, with amber beads as big as tangerines woven into their hair, and gold earrings that required a red yarn strap to help bear the weight, cheered on the bank. The first cows to arrive struggled up the bank. The dry ground was quickly turned to into a morass of mud as the cows worked their way up. When the last cow had reached the top, the youngest herder started to climb out until he realized that Baka and the other herder had turned to help the next flow of cows arriving. At least they could stand in the murky swirling water, grabbing horns of passing cows and turning them toward the shore.

For hours, the cows crossed the river, and as the herd grew on the tall bank, so did the number of people there to celebrate the brave feat of the young men. For some cattle, the swim across the river wasn't the worst part. For as the day wore on, and the tired cattle scrambled up the muddy bank, the slope steepened as great chunks fell into the river. Once they reached the top, the thick mud was like quicksand, and the animals slipped and slid. A crowd of anxious young men grabbed their horns as they struggled up the bank, for no one could really celebrate until all the animals had arrived safely.

Baka and his fellow herdsmen had changed into their arrival clothes, and as the last cow reached the top, they moved them toward the rest of the herd. Happy to have their cows safely across the river, they ran in pairs around their animals, forcing them into small, tight circles. Laughter and whistles filled the air, along with the melancholy moos of the cows.

With the night came dancing and flirting like Izdihar had never seen before. After watching for more than an hour she could no longer contain herself, and said with a tinge of anger, "Look at those girls. Some cannot be older than me. Their faces are uncovered, and their necks are showing, and they laugh and talk with young men."

"Iz, Iz, Iz," said the bead. "I thought we had already talked about you judging others. When you talked of wanting to live in the moment when all people respected one another, regardless of beliefs, I thought we had made a major breakthrough. But you still have that closed mind. Do you realize that a closed mind is often the cause of the wars you lament?"

Iz didn't know what to say. She sucked in a breath, embarrassed that Bella was right. "Oh Bella, I'm sorry. I am who I am and have never been exposed to such free girls and women before. Please don't give up on me. You've had almost 300 years to learn what you know, and I have only had one night."

Bella thought about that, and then said, "You are right. And I hear true remorse in your voice, so I know that you are feeling the challenge to change. But remember, different is simply different, not better, not worse. Simply different."

Iz took a deep breath and told Bella, "I will watch and enjoy rather than watch and judge."

Bella chuckled and told her, "If that was a question it may have been the one you needed to get home. But since it was a promise, it shows me that you are thinking on a bigger scale. I have full confidence that you will find the question that will take you back to Sudan."

The rest of the night Izdihar just watched the dancing and singing and feasting. She saw Marabout Karim sitting with a group of elders, sharing tea and a great plate of millet and sheep. He nodded repeatedly as the man next to him talked into his ear. There was music and laughing and festivities going on around the two men, deep in conversation.

As they talked Baka walked up to the holy man. He squatted before him, shaking his hand, and then touching his heart. Karim did the same. A man Karim did not know squatted beside Baka in the growing moonlight.

"Father, this is Amee. He is a Wodabbe, who are cousins of us Fulani. Their travels make us look sedentary."

Iz gazed at the man. He was taller and more slender than Baka, with skin the color of the dried river bank. It was a light brown, covering his long, thin nose, and high cheekbones. His eyes were widespread, especially compared to his pointed chin. He wasn't as handsome as he was beautiful. He wore his hair, like all Wodabbe men, in two fat braids on either side of his face, with another 15 smaller braids covering the back of his head.

"*Calmetevi*," said Bella. "Your mouth is open. It's a very good thing he can't see you!"

Iz ignored Bella and listened as Baka said to his friend, "Please, tell the marabout what you have seen in your recent travels."

Bad News and Good News

Amee and Karim shook hands. Amee sat just like Sheik Abdul in Morocco, with his arms outstretched resting on his pointy knees. He rotated a small twig between his fingers, much like Karim and his prayer beads. He cleared his throat and then said, "There is bad news, for there is war to the south and trouble to the north. They fight over religion and whose god is best. No one is safe, for even those on the river can be attacked."

He took the twig he held and scratched into the dirt, first up, then to the right, and finally down. "The river goes north and east and then south." He slashed a straight line across the ground, due east. "We must take a more direct path to the place you are going, which is the good news. Baka tells me you are a strong walker, one who never complains of the dust or the heat or long days of walking that stretch into nights of walking."

Iz watched Karim bow his head quickly, in acknowledgement of the compliment. He likes this man, Iz thought. She was sure she could see a glimmer of trust in the marabout's eyes.

Karim looked at Amee and said, "*Allahu Akbar!*" God

is great! "I don't know if my friend explained that I am a poor man, rich only in the wisdom of the Koran that Allah has blessed me with. I cannot pay you in goats or cows." Lifting his prayer beads, and patting his prayer rug he said, "But I will pray to Allah along the way, asking for a safe journey."

Amee tapped his twig on the ground. "We are not believers in Allah, for we have our own gods and spirits. But we are not warlike either. To each his own belief I believe. We welcome your prayers and will offer our own along the way."

Karim bowed his head once again, and then looked up at Amee. "And fear not, I am also not a warlike man."

"I knew it!" said Iz. "A man of peace who believes in a merciful Allah, just like Father." Moving the bangle on her arm up and down she asked, "But these wars he talks of. Nothing has changed in all these years. Why haven't we learned yet?"

"Learned what exactly, *Cara Mia*? Learned what? This could be the question that whisks you home, on a wind as strong a great *haboob*."

"I think I know," replied Izdihar, "but Bella, maybe I'm not ready to return home yet. Being an observer like this gives me the chance to look, listen and learn."

The bead was speechless. Finally, Bella said, "You are this close, and you refuse to take your question one step further? You are changing, no, growing my dear, and it is so clear to me that this Iz odyssey is not for naught."

Iz smiled just as Karim spoke. "My friend Amee," he continued, not having heard a word Iz and Bella had exchanged. "I know that religious wars are widespread, but not all of Allah's followers believe in war. Myself, I believe in the gentle side of Islam, where good begets good and charity towards others brings us closer to Allah."

"Not to worry," said Amee, "for Baka has told me what a good man you are. Wodabbe also share practices of charity and hospitality, and so I am inviting you to join us if you would like to. We welcome the wisdom you hold, and the spirit that guides you.

"We are nomads, living a hard but free life. Living requires unity, trust, and cooperation. Survival depends upon it. I offer to you these things to cross this desert." Twisting the twig, he added, "And we will travel well if you follow your own truth as we follow ours."

Iz gasped. "Did you hear that Bella — follow your own truth. Just like you told me, during the walk here. This makes me even more determined to learn my truth."

Bella was pleased and told Iz, "Now we are really making progress."

Amee reached his hand out to Marabout Karim. "It is up to you, which way you travel. As I said you are welcome to join us." He pointed at the river and told Karim, "Baka says you are going east, to Hausa land. You can take a boat if you can find one and travel north for weeks, and then east for as many weeks again, before going south for a long while."

As he shook the marabout's hand he added, "We will leave tomorrow night, before moonrise, after all of the festivities are finished. We have come to buy cattle to add to our herds of cows, goats, and sheep. And we have come to dance.

"We are going to Ayorou, a large animal market. It sits on the Niger River, so if your journey takes you further south you can find a boat there more easily than here."

Iz watched as Amee stood to his full height. Smiling he said, "I shall speak with you tomorrow and see what Allah has told you." He looked around at a stream of young Wodabbe men, all running toward a growing circle in the distance. "And while you pray, I shall dance."

Iz sighed deeply. "I am sure we will be walking again."

Bella chuckled and said, "Please do not despair. We will watch the dancing tonight – such fine dancing you will not believe it. We shall also watch the dancing tomorrow. And then I will take you directly to Ayorou, where my holy Hausa man makes the last leg of his journey home – by boat."

A Doctor?

The moon wasn't quite full, but it still illuminated the open African plains like a lantern. The stars glimmered softly, subdued by the powerful moonlight. And the night air was filled with a hum distinctly different from the chirping of crickets.

"Listen Bella, what is that?" Iz was walking toward the growing crowd that Amee had joined.

"That, *Cara Mia*, is the sound of the harmonious blending of 50 resonant male voices, humming in the moonlight. It is also 100 hands clapping in perfect unison, and 100 feet thumping the ground."

As Iz listened closely she could hear one clear, high-pitched voice of a singer, as if weaving its way through the 50 deep voices. "I wish I knew what he is singing about."

"I will tell you what his theme is, but not the exact words. Do you know that it is our friend Amee singing above all the others? To gather in such a large group only happens in this cool season, December to May. His voice, so high and clear, is telling all gathered to celebrate the two phases of Wodabbe life - hardship and happiness."

Bella was enjoying the lecture she was giving. "You

could have learned all of this had you wanted to walk, for Amee and Karim shared many secrets of their lives. One night, Amee told Karim, 'Hardship is the long, hot, dry season, with exposure to extreme temperatures. The shortage of food."

Karim had nodded his head and said, 'And even for those who are not nomads, it is the same.'"

Iz interrupted Bella, saying, "And happiness is the cooling rains that give us water and good grazing lands. Oh Bella, it's like all the other things that haven't changed in your lifetime. We still depend on the same things and are victims to our seasons."

"Same and not the same," said an annoyed Bella. "There is a big difference between a nomad and a sedentary person. Wodabbe life is difficult my dear. Family groups wander to isolated locations to feed and water their herds, alone for months of the year, in scorching heat. That's what makes tonight so special, for them happiness is the wet season gatherings to celebrate life."

Iz didn't say a word. She walked, silent and unnoticed amongst the people pouring into a wide-open space. They were gathering a good distance from the Fulani fete going on closer to the river. Women arrived sedately on donkey back. Each older woman was followed by her pack ox, draped in a collection of carved gourds.

Bella broke her reverie. "These ceremonial calabashes are displayed only by married women as signs of personal wealth. The most impressive collections will be celebrated in song throughout the gathering."

Still, Iz didn't speak, so Bella asked, "Are you upset with me for pointing out that your life is probably hard, but not nearly as difficult as the lives of these people?"

Shaking her head, no, Iz replied, "No, I'm not angry. I am just thinking. Maybe we should walk with them to this marketplace. I know that you spared me most of the march with our Fulani friends, and now I need to show you that I too am strong and can face challenges. Like dealing with the heat that also soars, by the way, in Sudan."

"*Calmetevi! Calmetevi,*" cried Bella.

"And we have known hunger. The rains do not arrive every year, and when they don't, we eat drought sauce, made from leaves of the baobab trees."

"Izdihar, be quiet please. I apologize for my shortness before. I know that life cannot be easy in the desert. But at least you have wells in your village."

Iz stood up straighter and said, "Fine. We will walk to

the boat ride."

Bella tsked, tsked. "If it is not I that has made you so snappy, then what is it?"

"You know, life with a well and baobab tree gourd is helpful, but still, I have many problems." Her beautiful face twitched in frustration as she said, "They want me to marry – soon. To an old man twice my age. If I marry now, I will never be a doctor."

"A doctor?" replied Bella. "You will be a doctor?"

"Yes. I almost said, "I hope so," but that is not the way to achieve my goal. I have known this ever since my youngest brother died, less than a year ago. If there had been a doctor, Omar would still be alive. I am sure of it. It's because of him, and my little sister Fanta that I have this dream."

"Are girls doctors? And exactly what is a doctor?"

"You don't know what a doctor is, and yet you assume a girl cannot be one?" asked an annoyed Iz.

"Is it like Madame N'Dour?" asked Bella.

"Most definitely not. A doctor has clean hands and special tools and pills. Many, many pills, and much knowledge of the body." Puffing her chest out she said proudly, "I have experience already, for I helped my little sister Fanta arrive into the world."

"So, what is the problem? Can you not delay your marriage?"

Iz twisted the bangle around her wrist, as far right as it could go, then back to center with Bella on top. "My parents are my greatest problem. They do not agree. Father says there is no money for school, and Mother says there is no reason for me to leave to study when I can be trained as a midwife right there in the village."

"Midwife — I know midwife — the baby deliverer. Karim had need for one for his wife many times, oh, but I am getting ahead of us again."

"My mother not only wants me to deliver babies, but also to have many grandchildren for her. I think that if I were a doctor, I could help everyone, rather than just mothers and babies. Boys like my little brother Omar."

Iz stopped walking. She kicked a stone on the hard-packed earth as she said, "I have seen and heard many things on our travels. Many things to think about. You have told me that I need a question bigger than me to get home, and I think I might have it. But just like awhile ago, I am not sure I want to ask it yet, because there must be more to learn on this trip."

As she spoke the intensity of the clapping and stomping feet picked up. Bella called out, "Let us go, for I don't want to miss any of it. You know me, I am a great lover of beauty, and beauty there will be at this celebration."

Wodabbe Beauty

Iz ran to the edge of the large circle of spectators. Men of all ages, on foot or on camel, were converging from all directions. Each was dressed in his best clothes. Only the finest flowing robes and turbans were worn, in all colors of the color spectrum. There were about 50 men in a long snaking line, facing the gathering crowd. Iz gasped, for the dance leader suddenly turned and faced her. At first, she was just amazed by the beautiful face looking her way, and then she clapped her hands when she realized it was Amee. In the hour since he had left Karim he had changed.

Amee wore a clay mask, spread over his face to lighten his skin. Iz noticed that the mask only covered the oval of his face so that emphasized his already high cheekbones. A long, painted white line ran down the center of his face, starting at the hairline and ending at the tip of the nose. Iz's eyes opened wider when she saw that his eyes were lined with the dark natural powder they had at home, called kohl. It intensified the power of the whites of his widespread eyes. His lips were also darkened for the same reason, enhancing the beauty of his already remarkable white teeth.

Bella called, "Iz my dear? Are you still with us? Did I

not say there would be great beauty here tonight? Look at them all. There are stars, circles, triangles painted on their cheeks. They are like Luigi, my artist. His imagination knew no limits in the quest for beauty. These men work hard to prepare for this beauty pageant. This extravaganza!"

Iz really didn't know what to say. She was in awe of Amee's beauty, for he really was a sight to behold. But she was also confused. "I have never heard of a man using kohl to enhance his beauty. Women, yes, but men - never."

Bella carried on. "Just look at them. The long, slender look of a narrow, elongated face. Brilliantly white straight teeth, so necessary to be beautiful. A lissome body complemented by delicate, graceful hands. The ultimate Wodabbe beauty also requires a long, supple neck, and wide, large eyes. You can see they are anxious for the *fijol* dance, only done at night I might add, to begin so they can display their charm, beauty, and desirability. I know how good that feels!"

"Oh Bella, please. I see all that. It is amazing. But do women really want men who look like women?"

Bella blew out a puff of air and said, "I hear the door closing of a mind desperately trying to open."

"Let's not talk anymore for awhile," said an

exasperated and confused Iz. All she really wanted to do was watch. "Please, can I just take it all in?"

As confused as she felt, Iz was entranced by the voices, the rhythm, the moonlight. The night took on a magical quality, as she whispered to herself, "I wonder if they still do this today?"

Bella felt compelled to answer. "Although tonight happened more than 100 years ago, I would venture to say that it still happens today. It is the power of tradition that glues together these unique individuals - dedicated to living free. I believe with all my heart that they have not given their freedom up. Or their celebrations of beauty."

"You really are taken with them, are you not?" asked Iz.

"I am, for beauty speaks to me louder than all other voices. So, like you said, let us just watch and enjoy the show."

Desert Dancing

Iz could feel the excitement growing, as friends and family members met again after another year of survival. New babies were proudly being shown off, and young men and women looked around with a casual eagerness for new faces in the crowd. She thought, here I stand and not a person can see me. It made her smile with confidence.

The rising moon cast a luminous glow on the men gathered in the *fijol* line. Amee, the leader, faced the line of excited, handsome young men. His voice, clear and resonant, rang out in the warm evening air, telling a story of the last year's challenges successfully met. The line of men responded harmoniously. Hand clapping began again, and the dancers moved forward, in a rhythmic two-step. Little dust clouds rose around their feet as they shuffled on the savannah sand.

Soon the line closed on itself to form a circle, and the beat increased. Small groups of men joined hands and moved into the circle's center for spontaneous dance shows. The clapping picked-up to double time, and syncopated, staccato claps set a counter beat.

Iz shook her head, for the wild beat reminded her of

Madame N'Dour and the sick sheik, and worst of all, the long line of slaves. It was as if Bella felt her thoughts, for the bead screamed out over the intense clapping, "Just think, you've seen terrible slavery and now you see total freedom. Where do you fall in that wide spectrum?"

"In the middle, I would guess. For no one owns us, and yet we are not as free as these Wodabbe."

She jerked her head up at the sound of ululating. High-pitched calls of "*Aiyeee, aiyeee!*" filled the air. Iz clapped, saying, "Here is another thing we do at home. Women sing out their joy in their own pattern." She threw her head back and let loose with a great, jubilant call – "*Ayeayeayeaye!*"

Bella laughed and said, "I just heard the mind door creak open a bit."

The women, all young and beautiful too, had watched the dancing and prancing from a slight distance. Suddenly they began to move forward in a tight line, closing in behind the circle of dancing and singing men. With the burgeoning beat excitement built, and the women began stroking the backs of the men as they danced past.

"I just love it. The stroke signifies approval. It says, 'You're right, you are beautiful.' Please *Cara Mia*, feel free to stroke me again, and show your appreciation of my finest beauty."

Iz rubbed the bead with the palm of her hand and said, "Bella, I know you doubt that I am smart, or that my mind will ever open, but you must appreciate me too. There are so many things similar, and I think oh yes, we're all the same, until I see young women stroke the bare backs of men they are not married to. In public!"

Bella answered, "You are right, I should and do appreciate you. And if I could rub you I would, so instead I will just tell you, - I know you are smart. I know you are curious. And I know that you have a dream. But I also know that you can be judgmental. *Mama mia*! If this is upsetting you then I wonder how you will react to the dance tomorrow morning, called the *yakke*."

"I shall manage, I am certain," said a really uncertain Iz. What could tomorrow bring?

The dancing lasted for most of the night, with clapping hands and melodious voices floating across the desert plains. Iz was sitting on the outskirts of a group of women, some nursing their babies and others dusting off their large, intricately carved calabashes. They each looked up, for another man had dropped out of the dance for awhile, to rest. There were always men who sang and danced, and stomped and sang, with no break in the activity until an hour before dawn. Sunrise found a quiet camp as the men rested in preparation for the dance of the new day, the *yakke.*

As Iz relaxed Bella told her, "Please allow me to explain what happens next. It is so wonderful, and if you know the meaning behind, the purpose, maybe the mind will be slower to close."

"Good," said Iz. "I like learning new things."

Bella's voice took on a quality like Amee's singing the night before. "The *yakke* dance, my dear friend, is a charm and personality contest. The key to success is facial expressions.

"Just look about you. These men who have danced the night through are starting their preparations for the *yakke.* I love the concentrated attention devoted to detail in their preparation. The choosing of most charming and magnetic individuals lies in facial expressions from well-decorated faces. Imagination is the key. Just like it was in my own wonderful creation."

Iz looked about her. No sooner had the sun risen, a bright orange disk pulsating through the cloud of dust from a night of dancing, then the men began to move about. Iz had eyes only for Amee as he applied a fresh mask of clay, painting again the elongating narrow line down from hairline to nose tip. He then added to his cheekbones small circles made of pinpoint dots. His finishing touch was dark kohl crosses at the corners of his mouth.

Amee called out to a passing dancer. His face was painted with star configurations on his temples. Amee told him, "Your dancing was very fine last night. What will you show us today?"

The young man smiled widely, his perfect white teeth glowing brightly against his darkly dyed lips. "Wait and see. I promise I shall not disappoint you," he said.

"And he doesn't," sighed Bella. "Look at his beautiful design. Creativity indicates such a flamboyant personality."

Iz held back a laugh. "*Calmetevi!*" she said. "Like you always tell me. Be calm." Together Iz and Bella watched the final touches in the beauty preparations. Gently sloping straw hats, some covered with leather bands and others draped in blue cloth were donned. One young man loosened his leather belt to drape down his thigh, as another cinched his belt tight, showing off his very slender waistline. The men put on their favorite embroidered vests, head bands and necklaces. Each had his own collection of long leather straps adorned with brass, colorful beads, and cowry shells. Three hours of intense preparation finally ended with a group of unbelievable decorated men. Iz couldn't wait to see what was next.

"It is so exciting," said Bella. "These men will preen and prance and strut to dazzle the young single women who have come looking for mates. *Mama mia!*"

Facing the crowds of eager spectators, a long undulating line of men formed. Quickly it took on a life of its own. Gently rising on tiptoe to add height to their long, slender bodies, the line of dancers moved toward the spectators. All eyes were opened wide to display their whites, enhanced by the kohl eye liner.

What happened next made Iz laugh out loud. An insulted Bella said huffily, "Rolling eyes, particularly in different directions simultaneously, are considered very attractive."

Iz was entranced, watching the moving line of men. They were clicking their picture-perfect white teeth in exaggerated smiles as they gently rolled their heads from side to side. They also puffed out their cheeks and puckered their lips. A low hum resonated.

Iz jumped when a young man, clearly inspired by the

growing energy, stepped forward from the line to display his charm and attractiveness. His head rolled side to side as his teeth clicked and his eyelids fluttered. Iz looked at Bella, saying, "I just do not know what to make of this all."

"Why make anything?" asked Bella. "Why not just enjoy it?"

Just then, the women, standing back beneath colorful cloths draped on their heads, stepped forward to assess who was the most beautiful. They watched the Wodabbe men preening and swaying, rolling eyes and smiling widely, intent on pleasing them.

"I like this," Iz suddenly said aloud. "These men are absorbed with out-dazzling one another, as they stretch their necks, roll their eyes, and click their teeth, all to impress the women. That is a change from where I live."

"At last," cried out Bella. "You appreciate a change. Now watch this. It is the ultimate sign of approval!"

An old woman dashed forward and bumped Amee in the chest with her head. "No higher compliment can be paid to a *yakke* dancer," called out Bella. "Do you now understand why I am so taken with these people? Our own guide, Amee, is given the supreme approval of beauty by the oldest woman here."

Quickly, another elder woman stepped forward and tapped another dancer's chest with her head. Excitement grew as chest nudges were given to acknowledge only the outstanding performers.

Iz stood there, jaw dropped. She hadn't noticed it before, but now all she wanted was to leave. "Bella," she said forcefully. "Can we go to the boat ride? I cannot stand around with all these women exposing their breasts."

"But they are married, that's why they are topless. Don't you see that all the young women are modestly covered?" asked the bead, still entranced by the activity around them.

"That's worse! For a woman's body is only for her husband. Please let's just go!"

"BANG!" shouted Bella. "For that is what has happened. You see only what offends you in all this beauty, not what has amazed you. That, my judgmental young friend, is the truest sign of a closed mind."

Peace

Iz gasped loudly when five hippos appeared ahead of their small boat. Their bulk was mainly hidden beneath the surface of the Niger River, but their massive heads with miniature eyes took Iz in. Then they quietly submerged. Tapping her bracelet, she said, "Bella, Bella, there are hippos. Are you scared?"

"NO!" was the only answer she got.

"Bella, I'm sorry. But really, me seeing an immodest woman is as painful to me as you being traded to Madame N'Dour was painful to you. I could not do it. Is it not better to leave than to be judging badly every married woman I saw? Please don't be angry with me."

In an effort to break the bead's silence she added, "I need you, for you can explain many things to me along the way, I am sure." She didn't mention that she also needed the bead to get home again.

Bella only hmphed, then spoke curtly, "Hippopotamus are the most dangerous animal in Africa, killing more people than any other animal."

"Did you say that to scare me?"

It relieved Iz to hear a shadow of embarrassment in the

bead's voice as it said, "Yes, I suppose I did."

"What will it take to make peace between us? I'll do anything."

Bella's voice lightened as it said, "Then you must promise to listen to all I have to share on this boat journey. It will take us eight days, and there is much to see and learn."

Iz thought she was getting off easy until the bead added, "And you must, once and for all, open that closed mind of yours. Because if you cannot or will not, I can no longer travel with you."

"I promise Bella. I promise to try. I must tell you; I am more disappointed with me than even you are."

"Well then, that is a step in the right direction."

Izdihar held her breath and looked at the bead on her arm. "*Salaam Aleikoum*," she whispered. Peace be with you. She let out a great sigh of relief when Bella responded, "*Aleikoum Wasalaam*". And peace be with you.

"Are we friends again?" she asked.

"Peace," answered Bella.

The Harmattan

"Tell me, do you know anything about this river we are on? Or shall I tell you what I know." Not waiting for an answer, the bead continued. "The Niger River is the world's 10th longest river, flowing for 4,180 kilometers across four countries in West Africa."

Iz threw her shoulders back and said, "I know some things. Remember I am the one with a map. Geography is my favorite subject in school." Loudly she cleared her throat, and then began. "It is also the 3rd longest river in Africa. "

She glanced down at Bella to see just how impressed the bead was. When it said nothing, she added with a slight bit of bragging, "For decades the Niger River was like the neglected stepsister, virtually ignored as exploration and curiosity focused on the Nile. Did you know that our mighty Nile – and Africa's longest river, runs for 6,650 kilometers?"

As if in a knowledge competition Bella stated, "Thirty Europeans died exploring this river. The most famous explorer of all, Mungo Park, drowned on his second trip.

"A combination of severe climate, malaria, the Sahara

Desert, and war-like people along its banks all contributed to its unconquerable nature."

Not to be outdone, Iz asked, "Did you know that the Nile flows south to north?"

"That's all very interesting, but this river flows in three different directions. Do you remember the map Amee drew in the sand?"

"That was a map?" asked a startled Iz. "I know what a map looks like," she said. "Don't forget, until I found you my greatest desert treasure was a map of many colors and all the countries of the world."

"Of course, it was a map. Amee may not know the countries of your modern world, but he knows the path that his people have followed for centuries, and the path of the river. So please, think back to the twig on the sand."

Iz closed her eyes, trying to recall the moment when Karim and Amee first talked. Bella's voice rang loud and clear as it said, "First he drew the line, or river I should say, going north, from Guinea to the famous Tombouktou, the ancient city of scholars located on the desert sands.

"The river flows north to the ancient city, then swings east along the Sahara's southern reaches, and finally turns south, through what is now called Niger and into Nigeria.

It finally flows out to sea through the Bight of Benin."

Iz patted her bangle. "So, this river is also a mighty waterway. Just not quite as great as…"

"As your mighty Nile," Bella finished. Irritated, the bead asked, "So shall we join this trip, or shall you just keep talking and bragging?"

Chagrined, Iz looked around. The marabout sat in the center of the boat, which was not much bigger than the canoe he had crossed in with the Fulani. Karim was listening intently to an older man seated next to him.

Iz listened as the man said, "Now is a good time to travel this way – when the river is up." He dragged his fingers in the brown water, moving swiftly with the strong current that had swept the Fulani cattle across. "You can see we are traveling with the current, and hopefully will complete our trip before the *harmattan* begins. We are starting a little bit later than I like, but with Allah's blessing we will finish this trip before it begins."

"Do you know the *harmattan*?" asked Bella.

Iz shook her head no.

"The *harmattan*," said Bella with a growing drama in her voice, "is a relentless wind that blows south from the Sahara Desert. With it comes a fine, red sand that stings the eyes and burns the skin."

Iz clapped her hands and said, "This *harmattan* sounds just like our *haboob*. Is it not the same?"

"It is indeed," replied Bella.

Iz shook her head. "We have so many things in common with West Africa." Then she thought of the old women wearing no tops, running through the crowd of Wodabbe men and shivered. "Many common things but many important differences too."

She ignored Bella as the bead blew out a loud breath. Bella said with a tightness in her voice, "But you still don't understand. Differences are what make us each unique. Which gives us each our own truth."

Iz didn't feel like answering, so she just looked at the 12-foot-long canoe, a small wooden canoe carved from a single log. Karim and his companion were the only passengers. The boat sat low in the water, the stern and bow filled with many heavy bundles of millet.

The two men were semi-reclined on dried millet stalks covered with a woven mat. Shade spilled for about four feet along the middle of the boat. A flimsy frame made from dried millet stalks supported another mat slung over the top of it, providing the shade. There was one man perched on the stern, wielding a paddle as both power and a means to steer. Another man sat close to the bow of the boat; his long legs bent tightly.

"So how did we end up on this boat?" Iz asked.

Bella sounded just the slightest bit snotty as she said, "Oh! So, you want to know about our trip here? The one you refused to make because of women not wearing their tops? Who, by the way, only bared their breasts for the special dance, not for the entire trip?"

Iz closed her eyes for a moment, took a deep breath to calm herself, and then said in an effort to change the subject quickly, "How is the marabout going to pay for this trip? They all look Muslim, in fact did the old man not mention Allah? Will he be offering prayers along the way?"

"That old man, *Cara Mia*, is Imam Omar. Before his death he was famous throughout the region as a great scholar and kind man."

"Bella, I love him. He has the same name as my youngest brother!"

"Yes, yes, I know that. Imam Omar is a holy man, also from the Hausa people. He leads his village in a beautiful mosque on the banks of this river that we shall see. He and Karim have many important things to discuss along the way.

"As for payment, you will not believe this. Amee, the Wodabbe, was not only beautiful, but also very generous of heart and mind. He and Karim became very close friends, on that trip that you missed. Once they reached the banks of the river again, near Ayorou, he not only helped Karim find transport, but also paid for his trip." Bella sighed.

"It was a beautiful thing," continued the bead. "Amee told Karim, 'Please let me pay for this final leg of your trip. You have been a good guest and fine companion, and I want to make sure you don't trade that beautiful bead away for anything but a wife.' He paid the man on the stern, Hassan, a fine fat sheep to carry the marabout home."

Iz's eyes misted with tears, so touched was she by the gesture.

In turn, Bella was touched by Iz's reaction, and said in a quiet voice, "And Karim has promised to name his first-born son Amee. They parted sadly, best of friends. I am sure that the unborn son will be the first-ever Hausa Muslim named for a dancing Wodabbe man."

"Oh Bella, I am so sorry that my mind snapping closed made me miss that."

"Not to worry," said Bella. "Let us enjoy this peaceful

journey down the third largest river in Africa. Behind you is Hassan, the captain of this canoe. And on the bow is Musa, first mate, if a canoe has such a thing."

As they drifted into the current Iz felt the rhythm of their stroking, and a giant smile filled her beautiful face. Rubbing the bead on her wrist she said, "I think I could ride this wooden boat forever."

Bella snorted quickly. "I am sure that there are a few things to come that will challenge you."

Iz clenched the bead and said, "Why? Whatever do you mean?"

"*Calmetevi, calmetevi*," said Bella. "Look around you. I have to say that I find this even more beautiful than the desert you love so much. And before I forget, did you notice that the most handsome, most imaginative Wodabbe of all called me beautiful? In fact, he thought I was so beautiful that he traded a great fat sheep to save me for Karim."

Another Trade is Made

"River life definitely has its own rhythm," Iz said to the bead. "Life must be easier, for food and water are within easy reach. Even transport is easier." She was watching long boats and short boats, all wooden, moving in all directions. One going the opposite way, heavily loaded with golden millet heads, and propelled by a man with a long pole, carried an old woman clad in bright yellows, greens, and oranges. Karim waved to her, and so did Iz. The old mother raised her hand in an answering wave.

"Did she see me?" asked a nervous Iz.

Bella didn't answer, so Iz continued to watch the shoreline. "I know that sound," she announced. Women pounding millet in their large wooden mortars were working along the river's edge. Behind them stood a scattering of square huts, surrounded by conical shapes.

"Those round little buildings are the mud storage houses for freshly harvested millet and sorghum crops," explained Bella. Iz didn't say a word as she watched a little girl bathe near the working women, a duck quacking back and forth around her.

The current moved them along swiftly. The rains of the

141

previous season were flowing down from the Futa Jalon and Mali. The skilled crew moved with strong, smooth strokes. Floating sideways to reduce their speed, then zipping around a small island and cranking a hard turn right, they caught the mainstream again below a group of rocks where the water frothed. Hassan, the captain, called out "Toh! Toh! Toh!" to set a paddling pace.

The day passed quickly, with Iz calling out again and again at the sights along the way. Large round rocks gleamed a bright black in the sunlight, covered with flocks of black African ducks and noisy Spur-Winged Plovers. Pied Kingfishers fished around the boat, suspended in air by fluttering wings while they searched the water surface below with a keen eye. Once a fish was spotted a direct dive led by a long, pointed beak erupted, and the graceful bird would carry away its meal. Iz clapped for the skilled fishing bird.

Both Iz and the bead had been silent for hours when Iz suddenly called out, "Look Bella. They are beautiful."

Scattered over a dozen rocks surrounded by rippling water and bowing green reeds, stood 17 Gray Herons, absolutely stationary. Some had their long slender necks fully extended in an S-shape curve. Others were hunched into themselves in a mortician stance. Still others held their wings wide to dry off.

As the golden light of the first evening began to glow across the water, they passed a village. The weekly market was just breaking up, and the banks of the river swarmed with a colorful beehive of activity. Long canoes waited at the banks, filling quickly with market women carrying bundles of cookware on their heads, and sleeping babies snuggled onto their backs. Every color imaginable was present in the vibrant splash, as the women clasped hands, laughing and carrying-on at the end of the main social event of the week.

Iz sighed deeply and so Bella asked, "Are you homesick?"

"Just a little," she said. "Seeing the babies snuggled on their mother's backs, and then hearing the pounding of mortar and pestle make me think of home. You know, that thumping greets the sun as it rises and sends the same sun to bed, everyday."

Iz watched the subtle sunset of roses and oranges wash across the open sky as Bella said, "Don't forget, if you are still in a hurry you can ask the question that will send you home. You were awfully close the other day. Are you ready to go?"

Iz shook her head and said, "No my friend, I'm not quite ready. I am wondering too, what is to come that can be so challenging on this beautiful boat ride?"

Bella responded quickly, "You'll have to wait and see, unless you suddenly find something else offensive and demand to be transported rapidly forward."

"I said I was sorry," whispered Iz.

"That's right," said Bella. "Forgive me."

The first evening was to set a routine that the group followed each night. First the men all washed and spread their prayer mats. Bowed to the east, they prayed in unison in quiet low voices. Hassan, the rudder man, and captain quickly began his favorite activity after praying -- the preparation of tea.

Bella decided to give Iz a lesson in tea making, so the bead said, "Only the green tea is used, prepared in a ritual fashion. A serious tea man carries his own equipment, comprised of a metal basket for holding the hot coals, and a tiny teapot that sits comfortably in the basket. Do you remember the young Fulani, Baka? He was the tea man in their group. They derived as much pleasure from a fresh glass of tea as these men. If you sit quietly you can almost feel the respect Hassan has for the ritual."

Iz watched Hassan pass the first glass to Imam Omar, and the second one to Karim. He passed the third small glass to Musa and took the last for himself. Hassan and Musa slurped noisily, enjoying the special blend for re-energizing after a day of rowing. "I would love a glass," said Iz. "But don't worry, I know that I cannot have one, and that no one could hear me ask anyway."

The night sounds were noisy. The air vibrated with the sound of humming crickets offset by the bass timber of countless croaking frogs. The two holy men were still chatting in subdued tones, as if they had not spent the whole day talking. Iz watched and listened as Karim took Bella from his deep pocket. He rolled the bead in his hands, and Omar asked him, "What have you got there my friend?"

Marabout Karim held it up, between forefinger and thumb. "It is my best trade yet," he said.

Bella interrupted with a shout of glee. "He has called me that before! Do you remember *Cara Mia?*"

"I do," said Iz. "But please calm down, for I want to hear what he says next."

Karim passed the bead to Omar and said, "My

Wodabbe friend Amee paid for my passage on this river so that I can save this bead for a bride price when I get home."

The imam rolled the bead between his hands, just like Karim. He then held it up in the full moonlight and nodded his head with approval and appreciation. "It is exceptionally beautiful. Have you had it for a long time?"

"More than five rainy seasons," answered Karim. "A woman, whom I did not like, gave it to me in N'Dar, Senegal. As soon as our deal was complete, I left for Casamance where I studied for many years with a learned scholar there. And now I have been traveling many months to return home."

Once again rolling the bead between the palms of his smooth hands, Imam Omar asked Karim, "And now you will use it for a dowry? Do you have a bride, or are you looking for one?"

Bella spoke up again. "Listen to this! I love this part."

Karim took the bead back. "I will look when I reach home. It is time for me to have a wife and children and share my new knowledge of the Koran with the people of my village."

Imam Omar cleared his throat, and then said with a

hint of shyness in his voice, "If you have no bride in mind, perhaps I have one for you."

Karim's eyes opened wide, and he said, "You have a bride for me?"

"Yes," said the imam. "She is my youngest daughter, 14 wet seasons old, and ready to be married. I would be proud to call you my son-in-law. How old are you?"

Izdihar snorted loudly and shouted, "No Karim! She is still a young girl, just like me, being married to an old man like you." Iz looked at Bella and said, "And you – you are proud to be traded to a man who gives his daughter away in marriage to a man he hardly knows?"

Bella snorted just as loudly. "And you, can you not see that a man of dignity and Allah is arranging a marriage to a good young man for his daughter? You are only thinking of you, and what you are running away from."

Iz took real offense at that. "I am not running away. You are the one taking me on this trip."

"And you are the one delaying your own return, if I am correct."

Iz closed her eyes and took a deep breath. "Oh Bella," she said. "I am not really delaying; I am just trying to learn as much as I can. When we return home, I must convince my parents that I have more to offer than just giving them grandchildren. Is that really so wrong?"

Bella waited a moment before answering. "*Cara Mia*, this is a trip to open your mind. Maybe you can see that what your parents propose is something that has been practiced throughout history. It's not something they are doing to punish you. Do you not believe that they want the best husband possible for you?"

"I really do not know anything anymore," said a frustrated Iz. "Please, let's just listen."

Bella had one more thing to say. "Well, Iz, if you can't be happy for Karim, or the daughter, then be happy for me. I will be traded to a scholar and holy man, Imam Omar, whose family will treasure me for more years than anyone else, from father to son, all the way to Omar's great-grandson who is Karim's grandson, Amee."

Marabout Karim dropped the bead back into his pocket. "I am honored," he told the imam. "If your daughter will have me, then you shall have this bead. And if that is not enough, I will do my best to complete the dowry with amulets or whatever else I can provide." Tilting his head, he said, "And I am 26 or 27."

"My daughter will have you, for she knows that I will

148

not let just any man marry her. I have not given her hand in marriage before now because I have not met the right man. In all my years gone, you are the best man I have met anywhere, including home."

"And the best bead," Bella added.

Iz just shook her head. "Please Bella. Let us just know that we shall never agree on this early marriage business. If it is not right for me then it is not right for any young girl."

Hippos and War

Sunrise was heralded by the roosters down the shoreline, and the pounding of millet. Iz could tell the men had finished their sunrise prayers by the little dust circles on their foreheads. Hassan was busily selecting coals from the fire for his tea preparation, and Musa reheated the rice from the previous night for breakfast.

Iz watched Hassan once they were back on the river. He was definitely older than Musa she thought. His face was round, and his eyes bloodshot. His feet, tucked beneath him as he paddled, were ancient looking. Even when wet she noticed that the shell of encrusted dirt and callus remained thick and hard. Periodically he shouted out a rhythm for the rowing, a staccato "Toh, toh, toh!"

Perched on the raised stern, he guided the boat moving swiftly along the bank. She listened to him sing quietly to himself, in a high falsetto voice. Karim turned to look back at him, and Hassan's face filled with a crooked smile that revealed messy teeth. With the paddle tucked beneath his right knee he readjusted his white turban, reminding Iz of both the young Fulani herder, and her father.

Next, she looked at Musa. On land he was a tall thin

young man. She smiled when she looked at his long legs folded beneath him. He sat on his tiny bench on the prow, his pointy knees up around his ears. As he paddled, he also broke into song.

"It's a sad song he sings," said Bella. "He sings of a lovely fair maiden, forced to marry a man she doesn't love."

"That could be a song about me, or even the imam's daughter," said Iz.

Bella let the comment pass unanswered.

As they traveled with the current they pulled alongside another boat, loaded with people. Hassan raised his hand and called out the Hausa greeting, "*Sannu!*" Hello!

Rounding a small bend in the river they came upon another market in full swing. Ten long boats were parked diagonally along the shoreline, like trucks in Iz's village ready to take on passengers. A livestock market filled the air with the bellowing of cows and goats and sheep. Off to the side there were camels for sale. A striking old man in a flowing bright pink gown proudly watered his camel at the river's edge. Iz felt a slight pang because she couldn't help but think of home.

Suddenly Hassan guided the boat into the shoreline. "We will shop," he announced to Karim and Omar. "If we buy enough food and tea here, we will not have to stop again, except for prayers and meals and rest." Iz leapt from the boat.

"Oh Bella, it looks just like our market at home. Not that ours is on a river, but all the stalls and action take me right home." The bustling market was divided into sections. One area was filled with men merchants selling farming tools. Hassan drifted off to purchase the much needed green tea and sugar. Iz followed Musa who continued past the fly-ridden meat section, towards the little piles of fresh fruit and manioc.

"We are looking for chili peppers, fried manioc, and a drink called *bul*," announced Bella. "*Bul* is a sweet thick millet drink that fills the belly for a long time and energizes with its lots of sugar. It gives our crew power."

Iz suddenly stopped walking. Staring at a young Fulani woman, she whispered, "She's beautiful." Her hair had hundreds of small braids, and her forehead was draped with a silver coin headband. Two long leather straps hung down the sides of her face, each supporting a shining silver coin. She had a large triangular scar cut into her forehead, and three smaller scars on each cheek. Her teeth were picture perfect white and straight. "I wish I was as beautiful," she whispered again.

"At last," cried Bella. "You can appreciate another's beauty with no judgment. I am sure she has rubbed a young man's back in the dances of our Fulani friends…"

When Iz didn't answer Bella added, "But let us hurry, for I am sure you do not want to miss our boat that is leaving soon."

Iz jumped back on board with a screech of delight as Musa stood in the water and pushed the boat, wetting his long gown up to his knees. As they moved into the current they pulled alongside another canoe headed downstream. "How is the route?" Hassan asked an old man in a tattered hat and dirty gown.

"The way is good," he replied. They cruised along together, exchanging harvest news and river news. As an afterthought the old man mentioned something that got a response from all four men.

"What did he say?" Iz asked Bella.

"He said there was a hippo here yesterday, but he's moved downstream. We may see it today or tomorrow. A lone rogue hippo, Mother Nature's most dangerous animal."

Iz shuddered.

Bella then added, "Oh, and did I forget to mention the possibility of crocodiles?"

"Is that what awaits us?" asked a nervous Iz.

"Wait and see," answered the bead.

Silence enveloped the boat as the shoreline changed again. Greens and golden yellows filled the horizon - rice fields in different stages of development. A singing voice from an invisible source floated across the water. Hassan, who had been quiet most of the afternoon let loose with a song in full voice, gravelly and deep, filling the warm African evening.

Suddenly, Musa yelled excitedly, "Hippopotamus!"

Iz grabbed the edge of the canoe as she looked ahead. There he was - the rogue hippo. His head broke the surface about 50 meters away. His wide mouth, stretched open in a massive yawn, displayed large molars capable of crushing anything. Snapping his jaws closed, he snorted a mist of water from his snout, and sunk.

Iz noticed Karim sitting upright for a better look. He watched the water surface all around them, clearly wondering just where the hippo would rise again. The blast of another snort located it, further away than before. "Al Humdillilai, Allah," said the Hausa holy man.

He turned to Imam Omar. "I have lost a brother and a sister to a hippopotamus just like that one. He turned over the boat they were traveling in. My sister could not swim, so she drowned. My brother was pulled under by the beast and died also."

"The world is a dangerous place," replied Omar. "I too have lost family unexpectedly, but to war. I have seen whole villages burned to the ground by warring armies. That is why I am going home. I wanted to spread the word of Islam west, but now I only want to share what I know with my family and fellow believers."

He shook his head sadly and added, "Peace is what this world needs, not men fighting." Still shaking his head, he continued, "I think the reason for the war has changed, and is no longer mainly religious, but more about power and territory. And to think, I lost two members of my family to that."

Iz rubbed the bead on her arm. "It is so sad," she said. "I believe Imam Omar could be talking about my country too. Right now. Why can we not learn that war is never good for anyone?"

"That is a good question *Cara Mia*. Is that the question that shall take you home? I don't think so, for you have asked it before. Maybe what you need now is to figure out the answer to that question, in your quest to return to Sudan."

Iz was startled by this, but not disturbed. "I think one answer is that if women ruled the world, war would not exist. No mother wants to send her sons to a possible early death."

"You are right about that," replied the bead. "But let's just enjoy the end of this day. By the way, did the hippopotamus frighten you?"

"Not as much as the story of war," answered a subdued Iz.

Brilliant Beautiful Bella

Mesas began to appear on the far bank as the day drew to an end. Their flat-top silhouettes glowed red in the late afternoon light, and Musa began to look for a place to stop. They passed a tiny village where an individual hut caught Iz's eye. It stood out amongst the other square huts because it had a triangular window, a rectangular window, and a rounded door. All of the other huts had a low door only.

The moon rise was early, and very bright in its 3/4 fullness. After a dinner of pepper stew made by Musa, the men all sat together, drinking tea, and discussing life. As they chatted, Musa explained that he and Hassan were brothers – same father different mothers.

"We were born on a small island that rests south of here, but before your village of Koso. Each year we travel north when the water is low, and south again with the strong current. This year, thanks to Karim's generous Wodabbe friend we were able to buy more millet than usual, to sell in the dry season." Smiling at a memory he added, "That fat sheep was worth a lot." They all gazed at the wooden canoe tied to the shore, loaded with heavy bags of grain. Musa looked at Omar and asked, "This war you mentioned earlier. Is it widespread?"

"Very," answered the imam. "From where I come from, far south of here, war stretches far to the west and south. Many resist the word of Allah, which I guess is their right. But it is a worse war, because now they battle for power, as well as religion. I have seen too much death, and so I am going home; to farm and pray, and to live a peaceful life."

Karim sat rubbing his bead between his palms. "What family have you lost, if I may ask?"

Omar dribbled sand through his fingers as he quietly said, "One brother and one son. Both soldiers, and two too many to sacrifice to useless deaths. It is because of them that I joined the army, and we went out to spread the word of Islam."

He shook his head as he said, "I was not a soldier, but a religious advisor. When both my brother and my son were gone, I knew I must return home. I also finally admitted to myself that if you are in an army, then you are a soldier, no matter what you call yourself." Putting the bead back into his pocket Karim said, "My heart goes out to you and your family. May Allah bless you all."

Omar bowed his head, and a thoughtful quiet flowed over the group. Iz gazed at the four men, each in his own world. Both Karim and Omar ran their prayer beads through their fingers, while Hassan and Musa relaxed, hands behind their heads as they lay stretched out on the dry hard earth after a hard day of paddling.

Iz sighed. "Beautiful Bella, Brilliant Bella, I cannot tell you how much I am enjoying this journey, but I am worrying again about my parents." Sounding a bit embarrassed she asked, "Do you remember when you accused me of delaying my return, and I denied it?"

Bella said expectantly, "Yes?"

She stopped talking, as if searching for the best words. Finally, she said, "I am feeling very selfish; for I am sure I have the right question, which can also be the right answer - that will take me home. But I am not ready to go home. If I am delaying my return, how worried can I really be about Mother and Father?"

Bella said, "Oh Iz, I know you know; I know that you are delaying. But I am so happy that you want to continue our tour through my amazing life. Please remember, for I have said it more than once, our travel time and your lifetime are not connected. So, enjoy yourself if you want to stay. And stay is what you want. It is obvious to me, Brilliant Beautiful Bella."

Iz had to laugh. "Brilliant Beautiful Bella? Just when I was sure you could not be more full of yourself, you show me how wrong I can be."

"It is our truths. Mine is to know who I am and how beautiful I am, and yours is to worry and doubt and judge…"

Iz could not accept this criticism, and blurted, "To be conceited is better than to be unsure? I am afraid I must really disagree with you now."

Bella replied quickly. "Confidence is a blessing. Doubt is a curse. You cannot have a truth until you have the confidence to accept it."

Iz closed her eyes and tilted her head. "Oh Bella, just when I think I am beginning to understand things bigger than me you confuse me more."

"Remember *Cara Mia*, we are searching for a way to open your mind forever. A mind that will appreciate difference, rather than judge it."

Bella suddenly snorted. "I just realized that you who has been disgusted and very, no, oh so very angered by sights of different ideas or ways, wants to be accepted for wanting something different from her traditions. Is it not amusing?"

Iz bit her tongue, for she wanted to deny it. Instead, she said, after a big swallow, "You are right. But I am trying to change."

"That, *Cara Mia*, is what counts."

Close Call

The scenery wasn't remarkably different from the first two days, but still it was remarkably beautiful Iz thought. It had been a quiet day on the boat. She enjoyed just relaxing on the fast-flowing river, watching the scenery pass by. The riverbanks changed throughout the day, from rice cultivation to rose-colored sand dunes that rolled away from the river. Iz noticed that one side, the east bank, seemed to always have more activity. There were men threshing millet with rhythmic swings of long sticks they used to beat piled-up stalks. There was a constant stream of women washing both clothes and kids in the river.

"Oh look!" she called out to Bella. She pointed at two tall Crowned Cranes prancing on the riverside. They were long and lean, with black and white bodies. A lovely golden crest rested atop their bare pink and white faces. They performed a dance as they walked in circles, bowing and strutting, then suddenly lifted off into the air.

Iz had noticed that Imam Omar and Marabout Karim were not talking like they had every morning and afternoon and evening before. Musa and Hassan were also more quiet than usual. It seemed to Iz like they were working harder each day – digging deeper into the river with each stroke.

The day progressed peacefully, with a long lunch and prayer break. Hassan had a specific place in mind for the night, so he and Musa paddled later than usual. Iz admired the pastel sunset that washed the wide sky, as their *canoe* passed two mountains.

Bella startled Iz when she called out, "Those are the Madame and Monsieur Mountains."

A large island appeared ahead of them. Hassan guided the boat into the land. Karim looked over his shoulder, about to ask something when Hassan announced, "We won't stay here. We just want to buy more sugar for our tea. This growing wind is making our work harder."

It was dark when Iz followed Musa ashore, but the moonlight was already strong. They wandered through moonlit alleys. The narrow passages, bordered by rows of mud houses, held the day's heat. A man led Musa on a dipping and turning path to an old man with sugar.

Satisfied with their purchase, they paddled across the river in the moonlight to the other shoreline and set up their camp. Omar commented on the serenity of their short moonlight trip, and Musa broached the possibility of night travel.

"I'd rather not!" said Karim. Iz was sure he was thinking of his lost brother and sister.

"Only for a few hours," suggested Musa. "But we can decide later."

The men had missed their sunset prayer, and each prayed in the light of the moon. Hassan made tea, and Musa fixed another pepper stew. Then they sat about quietly enjoying the gentle night.

Hassan, who rarely started a conversation, suddenly said into the night, "Tomorrow we shall reach a large village called Niamey. Do you know how much further south you wish to go? I don't know if you have noticed, but the wind is beginning to blow a bit stronger each day."

Karim sounded embarrassed when he responded, "I hadn't noticed the wind, and I am sure that is because I am not working like you are."

The imam added, "I cannot say how many more days, but if it grows too difficult, we can finish our travels by land."

Hassan would not hear of that. "We made an agreement when we accepted the sheep. If Karim wants to go to your village to find a bride, then that is how far we shall carry you both. Now I suggest we all sleep."

The next morning, after prayers and two rounds of tea, the journey continued. Iz watched the north bank of the river, where Niamey suddenly appeared. "Oh look," she called out to Bella, "What big, beautiful trees, although they are nothing like our baobab."

Bella replied, "Different but no less beautiful. They are mango trees, producing a fruit that refreshes, or so they tell me." Orchards stretched along the banks for as far as Iz could see, canopying shade spilling around the trees. As they drew closer to Niamey the shore became more populated. Iz was busy watching people work and kids play when the sudden sound of rushing water filled the air. They were travelling close to the center of the river, and she asked Bella, "What is that growing sound?" She noticed that even Musa and Hassan were looking confused, as the sound increased. All Iz could see before them was a flat, calm river.

A man on the nearest shore began waving at them with both arms and calling something loudly. Hassan immediately pointed the boat in his direction as the current increased and the sound of the water began to thunder. The men paddled hard to reach the bank, digging their paddles deep into the water. The man grabbed the bow as they drew near, and the end of the boat swung around with the current. He told Musa to paddle upstream to a small cove where they could talk. He met them there where the water was calm.

A heated discussion ensued, his motions big and expressive. Iz couldn't understand a word. Bella called out loudly, "We need to head upstream, against the current to where that large tree stands. Remember I warned about something you might not enjoy?"

Iz didn't respond because she was holding her breath. She could only think of Karim's sister drowning because she could not swim. "I cannot swim!" she called out to the bead. "I should have gone home when I had the chance. Selfish, selfish, selfish," she yelled at herself.

"Please do not panic," shouted the bead. "Have faith, but also hold on." The two men paddled fiercely to cross the river - before the current swept them downstream. Iz noticed that Karim's hands were grasping the edge of the canoe as Hassan chanted "TOH! TOH! TOH!" to set the paddling pace. The men bent into their paddles to get safely across. As they reached the other shore, again they heard the tremendous roar of rushing water, but at least across the river rather than in front of them.

Staying close to the edge they paddled forward. All saw the waterfall they had nearly tumbled over at the same time. The water frothed whitely as it spilled over a four- foot drop. Iz heard Karim's voice catch as he said to no one in particular, "There is no way that our wooden canoe, carved from a single log, could have survived such a drop. And it is unlikely that any of us would have survived it either."

Imam Omar called out a loud, "*Shukran* Allah, for sparing us."

"*Al Hamdullah*," responded Karim, Musa, and Hassan. The words broke the tension. Iz felt a wave of confusion. She tried to hide a smile from Bella, but the bead had noticed. "You enjoyed that? You surprise me."

"I don't know if enjoyed is the correct word, but I do feel full of life and energy, and relief. Maybe being so close to death can cause those feelings."

Rushing along with the current the men all spoke at once. Musa was the first to admit, "I was very scared."

Hassan shook his head in wonderment. "I do not remember a waterfall from before. It must be from heavy rains washing the bank down into the river over there."

All conversation ceased as they moved downstream. Iz was speechless, for the area around Niamey was the rice bowl of the country. Beautiful green fields glimmered in the strong African sunlight, and the area looked healthy and productive. As the sun shifted toward the far bank Hassan sang softly to himself in his falsetto voice. Iz gazed at the river where the oblique angle of sunlight shafts changed the watercolor to a metallic grey.

They were only a few feet from the shoreline when an ancient old man suddenly arose from the rice paddy. He wore a round black hat that matched his face. A white patch of beard contrasted with his black skin and hat, and his eyes had the look of wisdom and exhaustion. Musa called out in Zarma," *Mahteenkehnee!*", but the old man did not answer his greeting. He just stared silently, back dropped by the verdant green of the rice field. As suddenly as he appeared, he was gone. Iz shook her head as if she had imagined it all.

Everyone was tired when they finally found a place for the night. Hassan steered the boat between some rice fields, stopping at a large flat area bordered by the paddies in front, and dried millet stalks from a harvested field behind it. In the last light of day, a file of women walked past with gourds of water balanced on their heads. Young children followed behind, carrying water in smaller containers atop their heads. They all talked and laughed as they walked inland to their village.

Iz felt a surge of homesickness at the familiar sight. Bella noticed and asked, "Are you ready to go home?"

Iz just shook her head a silent no.

Beauty and Wisdom

As soon as prayers were finished and the men sat drinking tea, talk turned to the experiences of the day. Musa and Hassan were very tired, for besides the near miss with death at the waterfall, the afternoon had been the first day they encountered truly strong winds across the bow of the boat. The *harmattan* had really begun and created added work for the crew.

Iz had noticed that their paddling, which was always perfectly synchronized and splash-free, was suddenly messy. The flat calm surface had changed to choppy water and mini whitecaps in the afternoon. Musa's gown was soaked. Crouched on the bow he had been continually splashed as the day wore on.

This, added to the energy used to avoid crashing over the waterfall, had left both of them more tired than usual. Hassan made a special blend of tea, "To combat fatigue," he told Omar as he handed him a glass. Iz could see tired lines around Hassan's eyes. As the men relaxed the captain announced, "I am sorry, but starting tomorrow we will be traveling a few hours at night." He looked directly at Karim, who did not look happy. "It will be easier because of less wind." Karim just nodded in response.

Everyone went to bed early. Iz listened to the night that was filled with the usual chorus of crickets and frogs, and the sounds of a village across the open field. Voices carried in the soft African night air, and the nearly full moon spread an illuminating light across the land and river.

As she stared at the huge sky overhead, Bella said softly, "*Cara Mia*, you have a choice. We can end this boat journey tonight and go straight to Imam Omar's village. Or we can finish the river trip and go straight to Sudan after arriving at the imam's village. Please know that your choice cannot be changed later if you aren't happy with what you chose."

Iz thought for a bit before answering. "I do not think I will ever have another chance to travel on a river, so maybe I'd like to finish this portion of our journey." She looked at the bead on her wrist in the moonlight, and asked, "Are you suddenly worried about taking too long? Are my parents upset?"

"I cannot see your parents, but I am worried, about the time before you found me in Sudan. It was not a very pleasant experience, being buried in sand for more time than I care to think about."

"Why were you buried in the sand?" asked Iz. "I have wondered that more than once, but knowing you do not like many questions I haven't asked."

"That shall be answered in good time," replied the bead. "Ask your mother when you return."

"Bella, can a person have more than one truth?"

"*Cara Mia*, another very good question. Yes, there can be more than one truth. Just look at me — beauty and wisdom."

"Oh Bella, I will miss you when we go home. Will we still be able to talk if you stay with my family?"

"No Iz, when we return and even if we are still together, conversation will not be possible. So now you must ask all the questions you have that require brilliance to answer."

A smile spread across Iz's face as she began to nod off to sleep. "I think that will be the perfect combination — I can see you but not have to hear you admire yourself."

"Humph!" snorted Bella.

The Old Iz

Hassan and Musa, Marabout Karim and Imam Omar arose at sunrise. Iz stood frozen as she watched the rising globular fireball of a sun. The Sahelian sun, she thought, just like at home. She looked around, noticing that the sun was the only thing this place and her home shared in common. Her home was surrounded by endless hard-packed earth and sand. There was definitely no river running by.

As Hassan bailed the canoe out with a broken calabash, an old man came to greet them. Musa and Hassan asked him about the route ahead.

"The way is good," he assured them. Hassan wanted more information. - about the river ahead.

Bella told Iz, "It is good he asks so many questions, for he has not forgotten the waterfall yesterday. He is worried about more surprises, especially with the wind."

"No surprises," said the old man, "the river just widens from here to the next village." Hassan thanked him and then held his hand out to the two passengers. They got on board and the canoe moved into the current. The water was a thick brown color, and soon the far bank was half a kilometer away.

Iz sucked her breath in when she saw how far the other bank was. Bella said, "Remember, you made the choice to stay on the river."

Iz nodded as she answered, "I know. I know. And you know I think I feel one of my truths – I like to be frightened by new things."

"Frightened?" asked Bella. "I thought you liked to be offended. Remember the Wodabbe women?"

"Oh Bella, can we not forget about the old Iz?"

The bead laughed out loud. "You are so sure the old Iz is gone? Please explain to me, this love of being frightened."

Iz took a deep breath. "Think about how many new things I have seen and done. I loved our close call with death yesterday. It made me feel more alive than any other moment in my life."

"And in the moment? I am quite sure you were not enjoying yourself. But what is good is that I hear the door of your mind opening wider. I hear appreciation instead of judgment. Maybe you are right about the old Iz not being so strong. I was proud of you today, for not once did you criticize Hassan or Musa for not knowing about the waterfall. You only admired their skills that saved everyone."

Bella snorted as she recalled Iz's earlier comment. "But worry not, you will not have to endure my voice once we reach Sudan."

Iz said quickly, "Oh Bella, I'm sorry. I was just trying to make us laugh about something that worries me. I will always continue to talk to you, even if you cannot answer. For as long as we are together, I promise."

"That is very good news *Cara Mia.*"

Trust

The morning turned out to be a struggle for Hassan and Musa. The water was choppy, with a strong head wind. They hugged the eastern bank, which was covered with tall, sculpted termite hills. Neither man sang to himself, which worried Iz.

About midday, Musa began to look for a shady place to have lunch, pray and take a long rest. The river had not only widened to nearly a kilometer, but the banks were more like ledges than shorelines. From her position just above the water in the heavily laden canoe Iz leaned back to gaze up. The wide horizon had been replaced by a band of sky as wide as the river.

She could see that the wind was taking its toll on Musa and Hassan. As they sat drinking tea brewed to combat fatigue from the wind, the men discussed the need for finding another paddler. Imam Omar scratched his white scruffy beard and asked Musa, "Can we not paddle too?"

Musa's eyes lit up. "That is a good idea, but we have no extra paddles. Maybe if we find one in the next village you can help us."

Karim sat forward and said, "We can paddle, and you

176

can rest."

Hassan wasted no time rejecting that offer. "There is a fine skill to steer a boat. It takes practice. Are you a boatman? If not, then maybe you can paddle for Musa and I will continue to guide us down river."

"That is exactly what I meant," Karim said. "Have no fear, the last thing I want to do is try and replace you!"

Hassan's messy teeth appeared as he smiled at the marabout. Iz could see that his turban was wound more tightly than usual. The wind whipped the loose end until he stuck it into the folds of his head cloth. He said, "We must row at night, for then there is no wind."

Iz looked at Karim. "I know, and with Allah's help your work will be easier." Musa and Hassan looked relieved that all were ready for the challenges ahead. After a lunch of pepper stew and fish the boat crew took a long nap.

It was late afternoon when the group returned to the river. As they headed for the center of it, Hassan happily sang out in his falsetto voice. Their break had been a long one, and the wind had mellowed in the interim. Bella broke Iz's dream-like state by saying, "The men are happy because we are going to travel at night, and if possible, find another paddler tomorrow."

Iz liked how happy everyone looked. Omar and Karim were talking with much excitement, like they had all day during the first few days. Iz smiled as she watched the scenery. The river was definitely curving more often, and the banks had changed to great stands of old baobab trees, palm trees, and lots of little tree-covered islands. Iz clapped and called out, "Baobabs Bella! Beautiful baobabs."

The bead laughed at the young girl's joyful voice. "They are *Cara Mia*, beautiful baobabs, as beautiful as the wonderful me."

Iz did not say a word as she smiled widely at the sight of what felt like her old friends. A small village stood between two great stands of baobabs. Square huts and round granaries were set back from the river side. A group of men bathed leisurely in an open spot, while women and children bathed in another spot further down and out of sight of the village.

The sounds of conversation and goats drifted across the water. They had only been paddling for about two hours when Hassan called for a dinner stop. "We will cook in the last light of day, pray, and then carry on for a few more hours." With that he hooked the paddle under his knee and cranked it to the right. The boat smoothly landed on the bank of a small peninsula, where several young men were lounging about. They all gathered around to inspect the canoe, the bags of millet, and the two passengers.

Iz loved that she could look closely at them while they had no idea she was there. They looked just slightly older than her, with skin as black as the inside of an old cooking pot they had at home. As she watched them Hassan waded ashore and immediately began a fire for tea.

Iz laughed at how quickly everyone talked as if they had been friends forever. Bella told Iz, "Watch Hassan's face. He is not happy with the news. The young man speaking just said, 'There are small gorges and white rapids two days from here.' And Karim - did you see his head jerk up?"

Iz had seen it all. She did not understand the words until Bella explained, but she had understood that neither man was happy.

Karim swallowed then said loudly, "I am sure you will do well," to Hassan and Musa.

"That's exactly what Baka told the young herder," said Iz. Both men smiled at Karim.

Iz looked around. The land where they sat faced a wide bend in the river, looking directly into the sunset. "Amazing," she whispered as the sky changed from a subtle blue, fleeced with high cirrus clouds, to a fiery orange. Pointing with her bangled arm she told Bella, "Look how the orange sky makes the black silhouettes of the baobabs really stand out. It may be the most beautiful thing I have ever witnessed on Allah's big earth."

She turned to look at the river and saw one long ray, as bright as the ones in the sky, as it danced across the river's surface, lengthening as the sun moved earthward. The once-white clouds glowed with a golden light. Iz watched every second of the sunset show, with the bright colors finally fading as a spherical, nearly full moon rose behind them. "It is, I am sure, the most beautiful thing I have ever seen."

They were back on the river when the moon peeked over the trees. "It's perfect," Iz whispered to Bella. "The wind has died down, the air is cool, and the moon shines with the same power of a Sudanese full moon."

The men paddled and it wasn't too much later that Karim was gently snoring. Iz watched Hassan's face break into a moonlit smile as the little snuffles of Karim floated back to him. "Now that is truly a compliment to Hassan and Musa," Bella said. "Only a trusting man, a man with no worries, could fall asleep like that."

Added Power

They cruised until the moon was almost directly overhead, and then set up their camp in the light of the moon. As Musa prepared a fire to cook on, Hassan set about preparing tea. He looked at Karim and said, "This will restore the body after too much wind."

Iz looked around. The camp was near four huts. The rest of the village sat a short distance back from the bank. Beating drums and low-pitched singing voices came from the hidden village. Iz sighed with real pleasure and told Bella, "The moonlight, the river and the music is a great gift from Allah." She turned her head quickly, for when the drums stopped behind them, an answering drum and song floated across the river from the opposite bank.

Karim asked Musa, "Do you know where we are?"

Musa held his arms wide, as if encompassing the entire scene and said, "Somewhere close to Allah."

Not long after all the men prayed side by side, and then drifted off to sleep. Iz said lazily to Bella as she listened to the music switch back and forth across the river, "I don't want to let this day go."

Looking up at the brilliant full moon, a golden disk in a

dark night sky, she added, "I know I said the sunset was the most beautiful thing I had ever seen, but now I wonder. Is this not magical my friend?"

"That it is *Cara Mia*. That it is." And with that Iz fell into a deep slumber.

The men were all praying when she woke in the morning. Their arrival, which had gone relatively unnoticed in the dark, had attracted an audience in the daylight. One small boy wore a long blue shirt and no pants. He and four friends were squatting off to the side, seriously discussing the canoe and travelers. As the men finished their breakfast which included three glasses of extra strong tea, two village men came over to talk.

"Oh, oh, oh," groaned Bella, "Look at their faces, they are talking about the rapids and gorges to come."

"How exciting," Iz gushed.

Bella snorted and replied, "Obviously the old Iz is not talking!"

Iz noticed as soon as they took to the water that the terrain had changed again - from baobab islands to cliff tops rising from streaked red rock faces. Hassan called out to Karim and Omar, pointing his paddle at the bank they headed toward. "We will only travel and sleep on the west bank, because lions live on the east bank."

"Lions? We may see lions? That would be wonderful," exclaimed Iz.

Bella blurted out, "The stubborn yet uncertain young girl is becoming a daring young lady. Very good. It proves this journey has been good for you."

Iz didn't reply. Instead, she tilted her head back and took the sun and the wind on her face. The wind blew with a fierceness that really slowed progress. The men talked among themselves.

Bella whispered to Iz, "Are you listening for the rapids we've been told about?"

Iz nodded and replied, "I am also watching for the gorges. I am not sure what rapids or gorges are, but they do sound exciting."

Little curves in the river offered temporary relief from the wind, but otherwise the men in the boat were being buffeted by a steady breeze. Iz noticed how the sunlight glistened in the drops falling from the stroking wooden paddles, and that all four men sang different songs simultaneously.

Numerous bends failed to produce gorges or rapids, but the scenery changed constantly. Iz told Bella, "The banks look like they are from different countries." Pointing east she said, "Look, that side is brown, burnished and rocky." Then looking west, she said, "And look there – it looks cool with its lush greenness that grows right down to the water's edge." She tilted her head back and looked at the tall trees draped in heavy vines. "Is that what a jungle looks like? I have read of them, but never seen one."

"I believe it could be," replied the bead, "but I am not sure."

Large islands, covered with trees, dotted the river. At times Iz couldn't tell what was island, and what was bank. She looked up at the cry of a beautiful fish eagle as it soared overhead. And still no rapids appeared. As they rounded another bend into a peaceful little spot Hassan guided the boat ashore. "We shall stop for lunch, prayer and tea."

They picked a flat spot with a large *gao* tree for shade. Musa started his fire to cook a stew that he told Hassan, "Will give us strength." Hassan set his coals to burning, then said his mid-day prayers. After praying he poured a small glass of tea and held it for Musa to see, saying, "And this is a tea blend for wind and strength, so between your stew and my tea we will be fully restored."

184

The men slept for awhile, and in the late afternoon they got back onto the river. The wind had reduced, but still blew right into their faces as it moved across their bow. Bella told Iz, "I hope you are watching for a village as well as a gorge. It has been decided that a new crew member is necessary, so we are looking for a village. It was hard for Hassan to admit he needs added paddle power."

It wasn't long before we came to a collection of huts. As they approached the bank Karim said, "Please, all we need is one or two paddles. We can work, isn't that so Omar?"

Omar nodded his head in a quick little bounce. Iz noticed and said to Bella, "I do not believe he wants to paddle. Look, he is an old man and should not have to. And a holy man too."

She need not have worried, for Hassan rejected Karim's offer right away. He told him in a stern voice, "We agreed to carry you, not have you earn your passage by paddling. Please, let us see if we can find a skilled paddler."

Musa went ashore with Hassan. He was looking for a paddler, and Hassan went in search of sugar and tea.

Iz relaxed with the imam and the marabout. Rolling her hand across the bead on her bangle she said, "It is a great relief to be out of the constant wind." The boat rested right along the shoreline. As usual, a group of kids squatted down next to the heavily-loaded canoe, eye to eye with the two passengers.

Invisible Iz laughed as she said, "Everything about us is carefully scrutinized. At least everything but me! I love that they cannot see me." Before Bella could speak a very old woman, walking down the bank, came over for a closer look. She smiled shyly, showing empty gums. Her skin was old and wrinkled, but Iz thought her eyes glowed with the look of a much younger woman. The two men greeted her warmly, with much respect. She walked away waving and smiling.

Musa finally reappeared with a young man. "He wants to go with us but cannot leave until his eldest brother returns and gives him permission. He shall be here soon. This is Mogo, a Zarma, and he tells me he is a strong paddler."

Karim and Omar looked at the young man, then at Hassan. As he came up behind the two young men on the shore his tired face opened into a wide smile. Iz sighed and said, "He really wants another paddler. Look at his face."

"It is true *Cara Mia*. It is easy to read the exhaustion

upon him."

Bella's voice rang out in delight. "Karim and Omar must have reached the same conclusion, for they have asked the young man to come aboard and show his skills."

Before they stepped into the boat Musa said, "I should also tell you that he is not one of Allah's believers. Does that matter to you?"

The imam looked at Karim, who shook his head no. Omar said, "I speak for us both. We would not be learned men or good Muslims if we rejected another man for his tribe or religion. The world has many people that do not always share beliefs. Each should be able to follow his own needs and beliefs." Shaking his head sadly he added, "Finally I know this in my heart, for I have learned it the hardest of ways."

Karim leaned forward, extending his hand, and saying, "Please just show us all how good you are. These two men are among the best of river men, so you will not be able to fool them."

Both Hassan and Musa smiled. Hassan told the four men "I will cut a bigger bench. Musa is getting too wet on the bow. A wider seat for two will help immensely."

Iz looked at the small boat, already overloaded with

giant bags of millet that were becoming wet in the river splash. It was hard to imagine where a whole new person would sit until Hassan said, "If the two sit together, further back, it will more than double their power."

Hassan went over to a large tree, with several sturdy low branches. He walked around the tree pulling on several branches until he found the one he wanted. Musa reached into the boat to find the long-bladed knife and handed it to Hassan. He quickly whacked the branch off the trunk with several swift swings. He then marched over to the boat and wedged it in about two arm-lengths behind where Musa had sat the whole trip.

Patting the new bench, he said, "We will try this while we wait for the older brother."

Mogo and Hassan climbed in while Musa walked the boat out into deeper water. He easily pulled himself into the canoe and sat next to Mogo on the new bench. It was skinny and knobby but held both men. Iz sucked in her breath when she noticed how much closer the water was with the added weight of Mogo. She decided not to worry since no one else seemed concerned.

They paddled out into the river. Karim and Omar sat on their bed of millet stalks, ankles crossed, and knees bent.

The shade maker was gone. Its height had caught the wind again and again, and so all decided it would be a benefit to everyone to take it down. The two holy men watched Musa and Mogo find their stroking rhythm. Hassan sang out a strong, "Toh! Toh! Toh!" Once they reached the center of the river they turned back, arriving at the shore just as the older brother paddled in. Hassan had a relaxed look, obviously pleased with the added paddle power.

Another Wise Leader

Iz could see the brother was surprised by the sudden chance of work and travel for his younger brother. He talked to Mogo in a very rapid language that sounded like a backfiring truck in Iz's village. She winced slightly when she thought of home. "Bella," she asked quietly, "will I regret delaying my return?"

When Bella didn't reply she added, "I think there is a lesson coming. Is that true? Is Mogo important when we reach the rapids?"

Bella replied shortly, "You are always expecting me to tell you the future. The ahead time, and yet you chose not to return immediately. Am I hearing the old Iz?"

Iz shook her head from side to side. "No. Not at all. I do not want this trip to end until we have seen the gorges and the rapids."

"But you have seen the gorges," Bella said. "Those tall red cliffs, where the river ran so narrow? And the sky just as narrow above? There were also the wide gorges that you tilted your head back to enjoy. Those *Cara Mia* were gorges. It's the rapids you have yet to see."

Looking at Mogo, Iz told Bella, "Well I had better grow

accustomed to this new man in our boat. One thing is certain, he's happy for his brother's permission."

His brother had not agreed right away, for he was concerned about too much weight in the canoe, and how his brother would get home again. Hassan wasted no time heaving a heavy millet sack from the challenged canoe. The small boat rose in the water as Hassan slung the bag to the ground at the older brother's feet and said, "Here, take this bag of millet for his work. It not only lightens our load, but it also fills your granary. "

"That looks like a very good deal," Iz whispered to the bead.

The big brother eyed the sack, and then his brother's face silently pleading for permission. He nudged the bag with his big toe and asked, "And how shall Mogo get home?"

"If the family can wait, we shall bring him back with us in the dry season, when we head north again. But only if that works for his mother and father and you," Hassan replied respectfully.

The brother's gaze returned to the heaving sack of millet. It was a lot of food and would provide the family well while Mogo was gone. Slowly he nodded his head yes.

Hassan reached out a firm handshake to finish the deal. Without a moment's hesitation he jumped back onto the stern of the boat and the group pulled away.

She could feel the relief in Musa and Hassan. "They are definitely happy," she said as she looked at the tiller man's smiling face. Musa's back was also more relaxed, not quite so ramrod upright.

Iz loved that she could stare at a person who was totally unaware of her scrutiny. When Mogo turned to look back at Hassan, she studied his face. She told Bella, "I guess that he is about 18 years old." She looked closely at the deep Zarma scars carved into his cheeks until he turned forward again.

He sat next to Musa on their tiny bench, shoulder to shoulder. Iz heard Karim gasp with admiration as he watched their arms mesh immediately in a piston-like motion. Iz admired how their hands and crossing paddle tops never touched. A loud sigh of relief came from Musa, as his workload lightened perceptibly. Iz nodded and said, "It is a good thing he is here. Three paddlers are definitely better for Hassan and Musa. It's just like Hassan predicted — added power."

Izdihar smiled as Hassan called out the familiar chant

to his crew. She suddenly told the bead, "You know, he reminds me of Baka and what a wise leader he was. Remember how Baka led the Fulani herders to volunteer because he did not order or press them? Hassan did the same, leaving the final decision entirely up to the big brother, respectfully." She nodded her head and whispered, "I like that style. Humble but powerful and so far, successful every time."

Bella whooped for joy. "You have got it right *Cara Mia*. You need to only carry this logic one step further and you will be reunited with your mother and father. Are you ready to return home?"

Then, before Iz could answer the first question, Bella asked, "And will you apply this style you like so much when you get home, which could be very soon."

Iz laughed and replied, dragging her fingers in the fast-moving brown water. "It is funny. Before I was the one in such a hurry to return, and now you are the one more than ready. It shows well how quickly life can change."

She had no idea how prophetic her words would turn out to be.

The Odyssey of Iz

Iz's high cheekbones glowed with a fine reddish tint. Bella called out, "You are the sunset tonight *Cara Mia*. My dear, your cheeks and smile mirror the colors of the sky. *Molta bella!*"

"Did you just call me very beautiful?" Iz sucked in her breath, savoring the compliment. "Oh Bella, every time I start to doubt myself Allah sends me a sign that I have made the right choice to stay. And now, just think, a bead that is certain it is the most beautiful object on Allah's large earth has called me very beautiful!"

Bella laughed. "But why not? Have I not told you time and again that I appreciate beauty, in all of its forms. You are becoming more beautiful with each day, and with each opening crack of the closed mind door."

The bead carried on, "Is it not true that the old Iz rarely visits? Is this not because I am taking you on a voyage of a lifetime? *Mama mia!* We'll call it The Odyssey Iz!"

Iz chuckled at the bead's announcement. "I like that," she said, "for an odyssey through time and Africa is what we are on. Oh Bella, I don't know if I will ever be able to thank you enough for this."

Bella did her best to sound humble as it said, "It's nothing but a pleasure *Cara Mia*. Or at least now it is a pleasure as you grow and accept, and know different is just that, different. Do you have any questions for my wisdom?"

Iz sat still. She was watching another spectacular sunset light show. The river glowed golden again in a sky emanating bright orange and red rays. A formation of white-faced tree ducks flew past, honking on their way south. The group stopped for sunset prayers, and a cold dinner left over from lunch. The three paddlers drank tea, then Karim and Omar enjoyed three small glasses each before they all eagerly got back into the boat for another moonlight cruise.

Iz nodded slightly as she watched Karim. "He was a bit like the old Iz, afraid at first of traveling at night. Just like I was afraid of just about everything."

Bella interrupted her saying, "You mean afraid of new cultures and new ways? I must admit though, that even I was frightened by Madame N'Dour."

Smiling as she looked at Karim, Iz said, "And now, he rides with pleasure, just like I do."

"You are lucky to have an example of your growth, for you are right, he has changed. And you know - Omar is to him what I am to you – wisdom."

Iz did not reply. It got chilly at night on the river, and so she hunched down to stay warmer. Her legs were covered with a prayer mat, and her feet were tucked into the half gourd Hassan used to bail the boat out at every stop. They hadn't gone far when Iz suddenly began to scream and shift wildly in the boat.

She shrieked and squirmed and threw her hands in the air. Bella screamed just as frantically, "What? What *Cara Mia?*"

Bella shuddered when Iz yelled, "Serpent, serpent! It must have climbed into the boat during our last stop."

Bella called out, "*Calmetevi. Calmetevi!*" The bead suddenly laughed out loud when it saw what the problem was. "Look *Cara Mia*, it is not a snake. Musa had just pushed the long-bladed knife back and it hit a long-dried millet stalk that rubbed your leg."

Iz looked at the millet stalk resting against her ankle, and then at Bella. They both broke out in a great peel of laughter once Iz was certain that there was no snake in the boat.

Bella laughed and laughed, then finally said, "Oh my. You should be very happy that you are invisible. If you were real you would have certainly tipped this canoe over. And the men would have had a great laugh, as good as us, at your panic for nothing."

Almost as an afterthought Bella asked, "Just when we were talking about how brave you have become. Is that not funny?"

"No, it is not funny," snapped Iz. "I want adventure, but you saw me in Marrakech and the snake there. I fear snakes more than just about anything – maybe even more than early marriage. And believe me, I really do not like close encounters with snakes, especially while in a floating canoe, cruising down the center of the Niger River at night."

She had completely run out of breath by the time she finished.

Tension

Night cruising definitely had its advantages, for the men weren't exposed to the hot sun, and the wind had died down completely. Iz laughed at how Karim had first been very unhappy about traveling at night. Now he was as relaxed as a man could be in a 16-foot canoe with four other men.

Above the singing voices of Musa and Hassan, Karim called out, "My friends, I would like to offer a special thanks to Allah for this wonderful trip. And I would also like to ask Allah to welcome Mogo to our canoe."

Imam Omar smiled widely, as did Hassan. Musa looked back at the marabout with a smile and nod. Iz noticed that Mogo said nothing, neither good nor bad. He just looked forward and dug his paddle into the water. Musa tapped him with his elbow and asked, "And you Mogo, do you welcome this prayer?"

It was clear to Iz that the young man was unhappy. Finally. he said haltingly, "And if I say no will you make me leave the boat?"

The imam could not stop himself from asking, "But who refuses a welcoming and thanking prayer?"

"I do," said the young Zarma man. "I have been told many times by men with large knives and sabers that I must follow the path of Islam. That my gods are worthless." He snuck a quick glance over his shoulder at the older man. "We have lost village people to different armies of Allah."

Imam Omar dropped his head and fingered his prayer beads rapidly. Finally, he looked up and said, "I am sure you have, but please let us pray for a safe journey, and let us thank Allah for your arrival. Please, pray to your gods for the same, or whatever you would like."

Musa was staring at the paddler next to him. His face was filled with many emotions, one after the other. First Musa had looked very happy. Then surprised. And now angry. "If the holy men cannot thank Allah for our safe journey, then maybe you should leave us at the end of the night paddle."

Iz knew that all could feel the new tension between the two seated on the tiny branch bench. Suddenly Karim cleared his throat and said, "Allah we thank you for this journey that has brought many strangers together who are growing to be friends."

Musa explained to Mogo exactly what the marabout had said. Mogo looked back over his shoulder to Karim and said, "I have thanked my gods also."

Hassan started chanting "Toh! Toh! Toh!" and Iz was sure that he was trying to reduce the tension. Musa dug deep with his paddle, more than necessary. Finally, he stopped paddling and said, "I thought that we would be friends, but now I am not so sure."

Mogo shrugged his shoulders as a reply.

Not long after, Hassan steered the boat to the bank of the river. Sounds from a neighboring village drifted in the moonlight. The five men were quieter than other nights, and Iz was surprised when Hassan did not make tea after their final prayers. She rubbed the bead on her bangle and said, "Oh Bella, I do not like it like this. Why did Mogo reject the offer of a quick prayer? And worse, why did he turn his back to the others as they prayed?"

She thought back to the Fulani and the lone Hausa holy man, Karim. They had gone on with their business while he prayed. Somehow, she felt it was different with Mogo. His rigid back and little puff of breath sent a message of disrespect.

"Have you forgotten *Cara Mia* that many people, in fact most people do not always appreciate different ways? The little problem called a closed mind?"

"I know you mean me," she answered.

Bella made her smile when it said, "But that was the Old Iz."

Soon after the snores of five men filled the air.

You Saved My Life

"We call this place Karoga," said the old man talking to Hassan at daybreak. The village was already full of activity at sunrise. All 15 huts had spilled forth numerous children and adults. The women that weren't pounding millet were sweeping clean the dirt in front of their huts. A group of village men had wandered over to talk with the strangers.

"How far are you going?" asked another old man.

Hassan looked at Imam Omar, who quickly said, "My village of Koso is not so far from here."

"I know Koso," said the elder. "It is not so far from all the bends in the river that you will find today."

Iz clapped and said, "Oh Bella, do we find the rapids today? I cannot wait."

"I look forward to hearing how you feel at the end of the day," the bead said mysteriously.

Hassan fixed another special brew of tea, this time telling Karim and Omar, Musa and Mogo, "This blend is for smooth paddling and peaceful feelings. We must work together to survive this river."

The three Muslim men replied with "*Al Hamdillilai Allah*," while Mogo smiled shyly and nodded his head. Iz

202

felt relief at the smile, and Musa must have also, for he patted Mogo on the back and pointed to their bench. "Do you wish to change sides today?"

Mogo replied, "I am happy to sit wherever you tell me."

Iz watched as everyone climbed into the canoe in their same places. Three villagers pushed them out into the current as Bella said, "*Cara Mia*, I must tell you something. Today could be our last day on the river."

"Then I really need to see these things called rapids," replied an eager Iz.

Early in the morning sunlight the boatload of men, millet and an invisible Iz moved swiftly down the river. As the sun climbed toward midday, they came to the beginning of the tight river bends. A large rock face suddenly loomed ahead, and the boat made a jerky, tight turn to the right. It was the first real turn in the river after days of travel. Iz shrieked with pleasure as the boat seemed to skid along the water's surface.

She grasped the edges of the canoe as the boat fish-tailed its way past rocks sticking up out of the water. Hassan shouted out the paddling command, and Musa and Mogo each concentrated on his paddle. White-topped water like she hadn't seen since the waterfall cascaded around them. She looked back at Hassan. Iz thought the muscles of his arms looked as hard as rocks, as he quickly shifted his paddle from left to right.

Musa and Mogo dug deep into the water, doing their best to help Hassan keep the canoe from crashing into the submerged rocks. The wind was blowing hard against them, and Hassan's turban flapped in the strong breeze.

Iz yelled with glee as the boat rounded another bend. The change in direction sheltered them from the wind, but not for long. As they took the third turn, the wind came back onto the small boat's nose and sent it shifting out of control. Musa leaned into his paddle at just the wrong moment, and Iz's shouts of joy turned to screams of fear.

Musa fell overboard with a great splash. He surfaced with total fear stretched across his face, flailing his arms. Before the current carried them away, Mogo leaned across the small tree bench and held his paddle out to a panicking Musa. Iz's eyes filled with tears as she watched him struggle to reach the paddle. When it looked like it was all too late, Mogo stretched out over the water, his paddle just in reach of the desperately frightened man.

Iz shouted, "Grab it Musa! Hang on my fiend!"

The current tried to rip the paddle from Musa's hands as Mogo pulled it toward him. Hand over hand he pulled the exhausted Musa closer to the boat. Both Karim and Omar knelt and stretched as far out as they could, finally each taking a hand of the exhausted man.

No sooner had they grabbed Musa's hands then Mogo turned back to paddling. Hassan was wrenching his paddle under his knee, leaning left to guide them through the fast-flowing waters. His job was even more difficult as he tried his best to steer wide enough from the rocks to keep his brother Musa out of danger.

Tears streamed down Iz's cheeks as she watched the frightened Musa bob up and then go under in the raging river. Omar and Karim each held an arm now, around the elbow, bringing him closer to the canoe. Every time his face appeared his eyes bulged from his head, until suddenly it looked as if he was giving up.

"Live," cried Iz. "Please live."

She watched as the boat took another turn and once again, they were sheltered from the wind. Hassan steered the canoe toward a rocky point. "It looks dangerous, but what choice does he have?" she yelled at Bella.

Just then Mogo dropped his paddle. Grabbing the arm

Omar held, he shouted to the holy man, "You paddle, and move as far to the other side of the boat as you can. Take Karim with you. For balance."

The boat tipped and took on water as Mogo grabbed a limp Musa and hauled him into the boat. It was not a moment too soon for a loud screech filled the air as the canoe ground to a halt on the rocky beach.

Silence followed. Hassan jumped from his place on the stern and helped Mogo carry Musa from the boat and lay him on the ground. Both holy men bent in prayer, and Iz cried. The soft voices of the two men in earnest prayer were the only sound until Musa began to cough. Hassan rolled him to his side as water spilled from his mouth. Mogo watched silently, a smile creeping over his face when Musa looked at him.

Musa's voice was raspy as he said, "Thank you my friend. You saved my life."

Amee

No one spoke, and then they all did at once. Imam Omar was praying loudly, and Marabout Karim was at his side, also calling out to Allah. Hassan just sat with his younger brother, patting his arm while saying, "That was too close. We have a debt forever to our young Zarma friend."

Mogo smiled and said, "You owe me nothing. I did what your Allah and my gods wanted, which was help a drowning man." He dropped his head, embarrassed by the praise. "And now I would like to apologize for my behavior last night. It is as the holy men say, a man should not be judged by his people or religion."

Iz still had trouble talking, so scared had she been by it all. Finally, she told Bella, "That was the most frightening thing I have ever seen. It was even more frightening than when I helped my mother with baby Fanta's arrival."

Bella was breathless. "It was much worse this second time around. But look, two men who thought they would never be friends are just that – for life."

"Oh Bella, maybe it is time to go home."

"It is up to you *Cara Mia*. Do you have the right

question, or should I say the right answer? And if you do, are you ready to say it?"

Bella added, "I guess you did not enjoy the rapids?"

She silently shook her head no. Iz closed her eyes and said, "It is sad to leave them. If we go now, do we go to the village of Koso first, or straight to Sudan?"

"Have you forgotten what our deal was? The river trip and then back to your family, or the village and then back to Sudan."

"I know. Can you tell me – or will you tell me - does Karim marry Omar's daughter?"

"Yes indeed," said the bead. "The festivities for the imam's return and the wedding lasted for days, with much music and fanfare and roasted sheep."

"And was she happy? The young daughter married to a stranger older than her?"

"Very happy," said Bella. "They had many years together, and many children. Karim took her back to his village where he became an imam in his village mosque."

"And you. Were you happy too?"

"Very, *Cara Mia*. Thank you for asking. Imam Omar kept me for all of his remaining years, more wet seasons than I could count. And then his son and his son's son treasured my beautiful self for many, many more wet seasons."

Bella's voice filled with pleasure as she said, "I was appreciated for all of my beauty every day for four glorious generations in the same family. In fact, it was Karim's grandson, Amee, named for his father who was named for Karim's Wodabbe friend that traded me for the last time. Amee was given my beautiful self the day he left Koso on his *hajj* journey to Mecca. His cousin Omar, who had inherited the wonderful me, gave it to him in case of an emergency."

Bella sighed and said, "You should be glad you did not make that journey. The heat was brutal, and the rains that all expected never came. Amee reached Sudan as one of three survivors from a camel caravan that had started as nine people. Thirst and hunger were responsible, for the desert between Koso and Sudan is fatal for many."

Iz asked, "I love that the Wodabbe name was carried on. And so Amee traded you for what? And to whom?"

"I too love that the name passed down the generations. And I guess you can say that I saved Amee's life. He traded me for a fresh camel and cool water and food. Actually, the food and water were more gifts in the desert tradition of helping strangers. But it was that camel that got him safely to Mecca."

"And so, who did you belong to?"

"He called himself The Sacred One. He was not the kindest owner I have had, but very much better than that terrible woman in N'Dar."

"It sounds to me that you were not happy with him. Why did you dislike him, this Sudanese man?"

"Please Iz," said the bead. "If we are going to go, then let us be on our way. Tell me what you have learned on this odyssey. I know you have the question, for you have asked me about war many times. I also think you have the right answer, but I need to hear it. Think of it this way, what is the most important thing you have learned that will forever affect your life? If it is the right answer, then I will take you home. *Immediatemente!*"

Iz gazed at the five men. Hassan was pouring tea for Musa, and said as he handed him a glass, "This is for recovering the strength you lost in the ordeal. It will make you strong for when we resume tonight."

Musa sat up and said, "Please give this glass to Mogo. He is also tired from his act of courage, leaning out to save me."

As Mogo accepted the glass of tea Musa said, "And thank you for screaming 'Grab it Musa!' And then I heard 'Live Musa!'"

Iz gasped, "He heard me!"

"And you helped him. Be proud of yourself, for despite the chance of having to stay here forever, you called out help in hopes of being heard. That was very brave."

Almost as if they had heard the bead, Karim said a hearty, "*Al Humdallah!*" Praise Allah. In the same moment Imam Omar cried out, "*Allahu Akbar!*" God is great.

As all the men stretched out on the hard earth Bella told Iz, "You should rest too, for you have a decision to make before they get back on the river tonight."

Iz just nodded her head, a real sadness lighting her eyes. She rubbed the bangle with her right hand, deep in thought. "Bella," she said, "before I rest will you tell me one thing? If I do not have the right question, or right answer, whichever it is I need to get home, will I have to cross the desert on the deadly caravan?"

"We both will," said Bella. "But please do not worry, for I know you will do well."

Iz smiled for the first time since Musa had fallen overboard. "I love that phrase. It is exactly what Baka said

211

to the young herder, and Karim to Hassan and Musa. And it was true every time."

Yes!

Iz gazed at the sunset, which was another beauty. The sky melted into a streak of luminescent pink clouds, and the river reflected it brightly. As dinner cooked and Hassan prepared tea against the wind, Bella said, "The time has come *Cara Mia*. Do we return to the river or go straight to Sudan? Are you ready to get back onto the water?"

When she didn't answer the bead asked, "Have you decided? Or are you still searching for the right answer?"

With a deep sigh Iz said, "I have decided. I am just saying a slow goodbye to our friends here. We have shared many adventures, but more importantly many lessons."

"*We* might be a strange word to use, given that no one has seen you here. But wait, we do know that Musa heard you."

Blowing out a long breath Iz said, "I have learned many things. Do I tell you all of them? One is bound to be the thing to take me home."

"Please, tell me one by one. Maybe each one could be what will get you home. But I will wait to hear each thing before making a decision."

Iz rubbed the bead with affection. "I have learned that

the world still fights wars over religion and power. I have learned just how evil slavery is. I have learned that the world also has many different customs and people, and that different is not wrong, simply different."

"*Mama mia* Iz, you have learned it all!"

"But Bella, I have not told you the greatest lesson of all. I saw *Signor* Castelli and Sheik Abdul share it, Moroccan to Italian, vendor to vendor. And Karim and Baka share it, Hausa to Fulani, herdsman to holy man. And Amee and Karim, Wodabbe to Hausa, animist to Muslim, and finally Musa, Hassan, Karim and Omar share it with Mogo, Hausa to Zarma, Islam believers to a non-believer."

With a final stroke of the bead she said, "Mutual respect. It may look easy when you see it happen, but it is man's greatest challenge."

Bella chanted, "You got it Iz, you got it!"

"But Bella, please wait. I hope to practice the art of leading by following, like Baka and Hassan. And encouraging one and all, like Baka and Amee and Karim. And I must befriend that poor Dinka girl in our village. She will not be so alone and sad if I can help it."

Looking off into the distance she said, "But mainly I need to do one thing, and that is respect all. If I can show my parents, I respect their right to follow their traditions, maybe they will respect my right to not follow. Just like Imam Omar said, "Respect others' right to believe what they want and need to do."

Suddenly the night was filled with a loud "YES! I love you Iz," shouted Bella.

"And I love you Bella!" Iz shouted back just before everything went dark.

Home

Izdihar felt a gentle tugging on her *towb*. She opened her eyes slowly, and there, hanging above her like two chocolate moons, were her parents' faces. She blinked, confused for a moment about where she was.

"Are you hurt?" asked her mother

Izdihar shook her head no, staring at the sun that was rising over her mother's right shoulder. It was huge, and orange, burnished by the dust cloud that lingered below it, along the horizon.

Izdihar shook her head again. Her parents confused and concerned faces loomed over her. "What day is it?" she asked in a whisper.

"It is Friday dawn. We have been looking for you all night." Pointing at the sky her father said, "They gave us a fright, but also showed the place to look for you."

Iz shuddered when she looked at the four circling vultures.

"Why do you ask which day it is? Are you not well? Why are you lying on the desert floor?" asked her father. He looked around them and added, "And so far from home? How did you get all this way?"

"Oh, father when Mother said I must marry I just ran and ran until I collapsed. I ran toward the setting sun with thoughts of leaving for good."

"I heard you did not receive well the news of your marriage, and I am sorry I did not tell you sooner myself."

"And I'm sorry I was not more gentle in telling you," said her mother. "After you left I thought back to my own shock when I was your age."

Her father lifted his eyebrows and said with mock hurt, "What? You were not elated? All these years later I learn this news that my bride was not happy?"

Izdihar laughed as she raised her right arm, and there was the seven-layered chevron snugly fit over her bracelet. She held it high to catch the light from the rising sun as it climbed into the sky, still lightly dusted by yesterday's *haboob*. Twisting her wrist back and forth as her amazed parents watched she announced, "Now I don't have to get married right away, for I have my dowry. We can sell this and there will be money again. I know its value in gold, and camels, and cures, and brides."

Her mother gasped when she saw the bead, and then looked quizzically at her daughter as Izdihar said in a voice that nearly floated on the cool, morning desert air, "Bella."

"What did you say?" her mother asked. "And where did you get this bead?"

"I said Bella. That's what I call this beautiful bead," Izdihar answered. "And I found it right here, on the desert floor. Bella told me you would know why."

"The bead has a name? And the bead told you?" asked her mother. "Are you sure you are well? Did you bump your head or something?" Then her mother took Izdihar's hand in hers and gazed at the bead as she said, "The chevron – the aristocrat of beads."

Izdihar took the bangle from her arm and worked the bead free. "You must hold it," she said. "Feel its power and tell me why it was here."

Gently she dropped the bead in her mother's hand, who immediately held it high, between her thumb and forefinger, just like Luigi and Signor Castelli, the Sheik and Madame N'Dour. Baka the Fulani and Amee the Wodabbe had all done the same. Just like Iz had done. Then she flashed onto Imam Omar's face when he received it as the main part of his daughter's dowry from Marabout Karim. Over the years the beauty never failed to surprise one, she thought, as she watched her mother count the layers.

Sucking in her breath her mother whispered, "Seven

layers. The best of the best."

Izdihar giggled, for she knew if she could hear Bella the bead would be chortling with delight at her mother's description.

"And 16 points! This is a rare find!" exclaimed her mother, just like *Signor* Castelli had. Izdihar's mother looked at father and said, "We must guard this carefully, for Izdihar is right - its value is great. We will never sell this bead. All my life I have waited to see a seven-layered chevron, for my grandmother told me of one in her family many, many years ago."

"I remember you telling stories of the buried family treasure. How did this one get here?" asked Izdihar again.

"There's a legend I heard from my grandmother - that the chevron is so powerful that it just blooms on the desert floor. It brings health, wealth, and wisdom to the one who finds it. It is a great treasure you have found for the family."

Mother handed the bead to Izdihar's father, who had remained silent throughout their talk. His eyes sparkled with pleasure as his wife and daughter had their first conversation in months. She placed it in his hand, hers resting on top of his open palm. "You know, they used to bury these chevrons with their owners, as a sign of wealth."

"So that is how Bella was buried beneath the sand," mumbled Izdihar. "How long ago did The Sacred One die?"

"The Sacred One? Where did you hear that name?" asked her mother grabbing her shoulders. Her eyes bored into Izdihar's face, and her grip tightened.

"It's hard to explain," said Izdihar, wincing under her mother's strong hands. Mother looked down and quickly released her daughter, then asked again, "Where did you get that name?"

Izdihar's father, shaken from the sudden change in the mood said, "Is that not your grandfather's name?"

"Yes, yes it is, but how would she know? I never used that name because I hated it when he was alive, and so why would I use it when he is dead?"

Izdihar sat upright and asked, "Did you not like your grandfather?"

Mother shook her head no. "He was not the kindest of men."

Iz remembered Bella's voice saying the same thing. "Then how did he get a name as revered as that?"

Mother looked at her daughter, still clearly confused by

her knowledge of this name. "He gave himself the name when lightning struck extremely near him one day. It knocked over the teapot next to him but left him untouched. From that day on he insisted all call him by that name, and that he could do no wrong, for Allah had saved him."

Then slowly she said, "My grandmother, a sweet and patient woman, said the bead was buried with him when he died. I wonder…"

Both her parents turned to Izdihar, waiting for an explanation of the name. Staring at the bead in her father's hand she said, "I can explain how I know the name, but it will take time." Then it was like she heard her mother's voice again saying, "My grandmother, a sweet and patient woman, said the bead was buried with him when he died," and a sudden thought occurred to her.

Looking deep into her mother's eyes Izdihar said in a voice filled with awe, "Are you saying you think this bead could have been buried with our ancestor, and brought to the surface again after centuries of the *haboob* winds? Right back to the same family?"

Before her mother could answer, her father said, "If it's as powerful as your mother says, then anything is possible."

Bouncing the bead on his palm, just like the sheik did in Morocco hundreds of years ago, he continued, "It looks like that is what has happened."

Izdihar knew in her heart that the moment had come to tell her parents again about her dream, no, her plan, to be a doctor. Sitting on the sand, she took the bead from her father's hand, and rolled it between her palms for guidance and strength.

She took a deep breath and said, "Mother, Father, many amazing things have happened to me in a short time. I need to tell you all about it, but it will take time."

Stopping to clear her throat she continued, "I must tell you that I respect your ties to tradition. A wise man once told me that all must have the right to follow their needs and beliefs."

Looking up from the bead, first at her father and then her mother, she carried on. "Since the terribly sad day that we lost Omar I have wanted to be a doctor, so that I can save other children in our village from such a fate. If you must make me marry now, please, could it be to a man who will permit me to follow my dream?" She realized that she was trying to follow the example of Baka and Hassan, presenting a possibility without insisting.

Her mother's eyes had filled with tears at the mention of the young Omar and his early death. Father took his wife's hand and smoothed her palm with his own. Then he looked directly at his daughter, saying, "You are right, there is a lot for you to explain."

Looking into his wife's eyes he said, "You know, she really is a smart girl that should continue in school. And she is right; our village does need a doctor to help others. Maybe we can delay this marriage and she can continue in school. What do you think Mother?"

Izdihar's mother touched the bead in her daughter's hand and said, "Yes, let her stay in school for the bead will give us wealth when Izdihar is a doctor, and continued good health with her medical knowledge, as it now gives us the wisdom to know that she's too young to marry right now. Come, let's take our treasures home."

"*Al Hamdillilai Allah!*" Izdihar whispered under her breath just like Karim and Omar. She knew that the final word had been spoken when her mother said, "…when Izdihar is a doctor."

Izdihar stood tall as she walked between her parents toward the family hut. The sun already beat down on the three, who stopped once more to admire the bead resting on Izdihar's palm. She closed her hand around Bella and wrapped an arm around each parent's elbow. She hugged their arms with a quick squeeze, for she knew that everything was going to be all right.

Just before she entered the hut, she stopped her parents and said with much emotion, "I love you dearly." They laughed softly with a touch of embarrassment, then they laughed out loud when she said, "Oh yes, and from now on, could you please call me Iz?"

THE END

GLOSSARY

In order of appearance in book:

Haboob – (Arabic): The strong winds that blow down off the Sahara every May and June, just before the rainy season.

Towb – (Arabic): Nine meters of colorful cloth that women wrap loosely over their dresses, around their heads and bodies.

Hajj – (Arabic): The holy pilgrimage trip to Mecca.

Fuul – (Arabic): Fava beans cooked with onions, tomatoes, pepper and eaten with heavy chunks of bread.

Khalas – (Arabic): Finished. Said like, "The end".

Molta bella – (Italian): Very beautiful

Buongiorno – (Italian): Good morning

Signor – (Italian): Mr

Millefiori – (Italian): Medieval Italian for *thousand flowers*, so named for the colorful designs that cover the bead. They date back to 300 B.C.

Wadi – (Arabic): A dry river or stream bed.

Mama mia! – (Italian): An expression of surprise, both for happy events and sad.

Cara Mia – (Italian): An affectionate term, My Dear.

Lucha – (Italian): A fight, in this case over the price.

Ma scusate – (Italian): Excuse me

Cuez – (Arabic): Good

Inshallah – (Arabic): God or Allah willing

Salaam Aleikoum – (Arabic): Greeting, "peace be with you".

Aleikoum Wasalaam – (Arabic): Greeting reply, "And with you".

Buongiorno, cuez katir, ça va bien? – (Italian, Arabic, French): Good morning, very good, are you well?

Jalabiyah – (Arabic): Loose robe worn by northern Sudanese men.

Shukran – (Arabic): Thank you

Chai – (Arabic): Tea

Cuez katir! – (Arabic): Very good! Very beautiful!

Bui-bui – (Arabic): A black over robe worn by Muslim women.

Calmetevi, calmetevi – (Italian): Calm down, calm down

Gri-gri – (Undetermined African language, but common throughout the continent): Black magic

Juju – (Krio, West Africa): Black magic

Tristissimo– (Italian): Very sad

Malesh – (Arabic, ma-LESH): Sorry

Ma va!! – (Italian): Never!

Esatamente – (Italian): Exactly, precisely

Na nga def – (Wolof): Hello

La malattia – (Italian): The illness

Balafones – (West African): Wooden xylophones that use gourds as the reverberators.

Immediatementé – (Italian): Immediately

Al Hamdillilai – (Arabic): A variation of Praise Allah.

Marabout – (Arabic): A religious teacher, Koran scholar.

Numero tre – (Italian): Number three

Per sempre – (Italian): Always!

Sittasahar, saebae tashar, taemaentashar – (Arabic): Sixteen, seventeen, eighteen.

Djenne – (Unsure of origin): A major town in Mali, but in this case a type of grass that improves night vision.

Allahu Akbar! – (Arabic): God is great!

Bisimallah – (Arabic): In the name of God.

Fijol – (Wodabbe): A special dance done only at night.

Yakke – (Wodabbe): A beauty competition and dance.

Harmattan – (Arabic): A dry wind that blows down from the Sahara in December, January and February.

Bul – (Uncertain if Zarma or Hausa): A filling drink

made from millet and sugar.

Al Hamdullah – (Arabic): Another variation of praise Allah!

Mahteenkehnee! – (Zarma): Greeting meaning hello.

Gao – (Unknown): A hearty tree that lives in the Sahel, needing little water and providing natural fertilizer with the leaves that fall annually.

CRISTINA KESSLER

Cristina Kessler knew she wanted to be a writer at the age of ten, and since she was twelve, she knew she would travel the world. Not surprisingly, she put these two early dreams together.

A Peace Corps worker originally, she lived abroad for 30 years. For 20 of those years, she called Africa home. Her love and respect for the people and her personal connection brings an authenticity and life to her stories rare in children's books and young adult novels set in Africa.

Committed to sharing these rich cultures with her global readers, she has authored several young adult novels including, **No Condition Is Permanent**, a story set in Sierra Leone, the award-winning **Our Secret, Siri Aang**, a story of the Maasai set in Kenya. It won the Henry Bergh Award from the ASPCA for Excellence in Humane Literature for Young Readers. **Trouble in Timbuktu**, set in Mali, won the 2005 Africana Honor Book Award which is given by the African Studies Association annually, and honors outstanding authors and illustrators of books about Africa published for children and young adults in the United States.

Her most recent YA novel, **The Odyssey of Iz**, is a story of adventures involving a talking chevron trade bead with the power to travel through time and a young Sudanese girl named Izdihar. Cristina has received awards and special recognitions for her children's books including **One Night, Konte Chameleon Fine, Fine Fine!, My Great-Grandmother's Gourd, Jubela, The Best Beekeeper of Lalibela,** and **All the King's Animals.** Her only book not set in Africa; **Hope is Here!** won the Lumen Award for Literary Excellence for Youth Nonfiction.

Cristina has also traveled down Memory Lane and written a memoir, **Tales of an Ikut Swami**, a collection of her experiences with women in the Developing World. Each country was a new adventure and a new challenge and being an Ikut Swami gave her the freedom to try whatever opportunities came her way.

With her books for kids, she has a personal writing agenda, which is to get the good news out about Africa.

She and her husband, Joe, currently reside on St. John in the U.S. Virgin Islands, but she still misses Africa like she left yesterday.